CHARLOTTE PHILLIPS

I live in Wiltshire, UK, where I squash writing in between looking after my family, who have been taught not to notice that I'm rubbish at housework. I love watching American TV shows in my pyjamas and I can't live without coffee and cake.

Your Room or Mine?

CHARLOTTE PHILLIPS

Harper*Impulse* an imprint of
HarperCollins*Publishers* Ltd
77–85 Fulham Palace Road
Hammersmith, London W6 8JB

www.harpercollins.co.uk

A Paperback Original 2014

First published in Great Britain in ebook format by Harper*Impulse* 2013

A catalogue record for this book
is available from the British Library

ISBN: 978-0-00-755960-2

This novel is entirely a work of fiction.
The names, characters and incidents portrayed in it are
the work of the author's imagination. Any resemblance to
actual persons, living or dead, events or localities is
entirely coincidental.

Automatically produced by Atomik ePublisher from Easypress

For Fran, who is always in my corner.
With love and thanks.

CHAPTER 1

Izzy Shaw glanced around the hotel lobby full of loved-up couples revelling in the sumptuous luxury and wondered in what universe she'd thought a night here by herself could succeed where ice-cream, wine and support sessions with the girls had failed.

To pass the time as she queued for check-in, and to strengthen her resolve, she mentally ran through the list she'd made of Joe's faults, which according to her friend Shauna should be referred to at moments of weakness.

1) Leaves boxer shorts on the floor.
2) Watches more than one show at once on TV resulting in infuriating flicking of remote control.
3) Obsessive preoccupation with major football events plus outrageous cash outlay on season ticket.
4) Leaves toilet door open.
5) Has one night stands while supposedly working away.

Of course, that last one was the only one that really counted. She'd put up with all the others for three years, none of them had been deal breakers.

She reached down for the handle of her overnight bag and moved up two spaces in the line. The couple in front of her were so closely entwined together that she could hardly tell where one person stopped and the other began. As she watched the girl nuzzled into her partner's neck and Izzy averted her eyes and stared at the glossy marble floor.

Urgh! Get a room!

She supposed that's exactly what they were doing. Just as she would have been, in that parallel universe where Joe hadn't let her down.

A few nights in the company of her friends in the wake of her discovery of Joe's betrayal had certainly filled her with temporary bravado. Opting to take this night away herself as a pamper break instead of just cutting her losses and cancelling had seemed like a great idea when she was buoyed up by wine and chocolate and pep talks.

'It'll just be a waste of a good room if you don't go,' Shauna had insisted. 'You won't get the money back now. It's luxurious, it's expensive and best of all it's got the perfect access for Selfridges and Harvey Nicks. An evening in the spa, a gourmet dinner and then you shop until you drop. You'll be over him within 24 hours.'

The moment six months ago when she'd booked this place flashed into her mind. Just *great*. Because what she really *needed* right now was a flashback to a time when Joe had been everything to her. She gritted her teeth hard. This was her Reinvention Mini-Break, her Get-Strong Mini-Break. It was NOT the planned Izzy-and-Joe's Surprise Romantic Mini-Break. Plans could change.

People could change too.

She reached the front of the line. She carried her bag to the Receptionist and forced a smile across the high marble counter.

'I have a booking in the name of 'Shaw',' she said.

The receptionist pressed buttons, nodded efficiently.

'I have a table booked in the restaurant for tonight,' the receptionist said. 'And a His and Hers Spa Treatment.'

She'd forgotten about that. The lobby seemed suddenly too warm.

'Can I change the Spa treatment?' she said, trying to keep her voice as muted as possible. There was zero privacy at the crowded check-in desk. 'Something a bit more...' she groped for the right description and failed. 'For one?' she said.

The receptionist glanced up, clearly taking in the fact that she was alone. The warmth of a blush crept upwards from her neck. She might as well have stood on the counter and announced to the room that she was unexpectedly single.

'I'm afraid the His-and-Hers Treatment is part of the Romantic Getaway Package,' the receptionist said, not bothering to lower her voice. 'I can cancel it of course, but I can't swap it for anything else.'

Izzy stared at her.

'Of course, you're welcome to book additional treatments as you like, they will be charged individually. If you'd care to ring down to the Spa when you've checked in, they can give you a list.'

'Fine,' Izzy said. 'Please can I just get checked in?'

'And would you like me to cancel the His-and-Hers...' she glanced at the screen '...Massage?'

'Cancel it!' Izzy snapped. 'Just cancel it. Not a problem.'

She felt eyes upon her and glanced sideways. A few feet away a man was being checked in by the other receptionist. Standing out, like her, singleton among cosy couples. Thick dark hair, lightly tousled. Strong jaw. Dark suit so sharply cut it had to be crushingly expensive. Broad shoulders and a chiselled handsome face that had the receptionist fawning over him. Izzy registered the ghost of a smile on his lips as he looked at her, clearly listening in on every word.

Her heart, broken of course and so not working as it should, upped its pace in her chest because he really was gorgeous. In fact if her head, still channelling anger, hadn't reminded her that Joe had used his nights away with work to bed random women, then her jaw might have hit the polished counter top as it dropped. Was this how he used to behave – eyeing up women at hotel receptions, picking the perfect candidate? She snapped her eyes away.

Think about the shopping, Izzy. Think about complimentary chocolates in the room with no need to worry anymore that they might go straight to your hips...

'Would you like help with your luggage?'

'No, thank you.'

She didn't want help with her luggage or complimentary newspapers or to be stared at by other guests, especially drop-dead gorgeous ones with possibly dubious motives. She wanted to get to her room and pull herself together.

***

At last taking the keycard from the receptionist, she swung around, handbag hooked into one hand, holdall in the other, and crossed the lobby towards the stairs. A misjudged glance back, just a general glance of course, definitely NOT to see if Mr Dark-Tousled-Hair was still looking at her, and she somehow managed to catch her overstuffed holdall in the enormous plant stupidly located at the corner of the sweeping staircase. It promptly toppled off its ornate circular table and emptied itself onto the deep pile rug at her feet.

The buzz of noise in the lobby dropped a notch as people turned to look. Izzy's face burned hotter than ever. What kind of moron had placed a plant there of all places?

Exasperated, she shoved her bags to one side and knelt down on the carpet to set about picking it up, feeling the eyes of everyone in the lobby burning into her back. Soil dusted her hands and collected beneath her fingernails.

A pair of hands appeared next to hers and helped her right the pot and ease the plant back into it. Big strong hands, a dark-stoned signet ring on the left little finger. Surely too expensive to belong to the scrawny concierge, who had looked about twelve. She glanced up, straight into the hazel eyes of the man from the check-in desk. His eyes crinkled softly at the corners as he smiled at her and her stomach gave a slow and traitorous backflip. She snapped her eyes back down to the black soil littering the carpet and rearranged her face into what she hoped was a neutral expression.

Scooping soil up between her hands, she thrust it back in the pot, pressing gently to reseat the plant. The schoolboy concierge joined them.

'I'm really sorry,' she told him. 'I just caught it with my case and tipped it over.'

'No problem, madam.'

'It should be fine but still you might want to consider repotting it,' she added automatically, the part of her that spent her entire working life around plants taking over. 'It looks to me like it might be potbound – did you see there were mostly roots there rather than soil? And some of the leaves are turning yellow?'

The concierge stared at her as if she were an alien. Her shoulders sagged. Why was she bothering?

'Sorry,' she mumbled and grabbed her bags, leaving the remains of the mess behind her as she took the stairs.

She was a few steps up when she realised the man from check-in was keeping pace next to her.

'Thanks,' she said, because he was wearing a suit and still he hadn't hesitated to get soil under his nails on her behalf.

'You're welcome,' he said. 'You obviously know your way around pot plants.' His voice was deep and smooth. A voice that could draw you in.

'Not literally, unfortunately,' she said.

He smiled and she offered a polite smile back.

'I'm a gardener,' she said, turning at the first landing. He stayed alongside her.

'Really? You don't look like a gardener.'

'What does a gardener look like?'

He shrugged.

'Sweaty, old jeans, grimy hands, crack of butt on show.'

She laughed.

'Yeah well, it is my day off,' she said.

He smiled a delicious lop-sided smile that lifted the left corner of his mouth and crinkled the warm hazel eyes at the corners. A smile that had meaning beyond politeness.

Izzy looked away as her heart gave a skip of triumph, such a long-forgotten sensation that it nearly brought her to a standstill. *He was flirting with her.*

When had she last flirted with anyone? Three years of pouring herself into work, building her business up from scratch. Joe doing the same, working all hours, both of them with their shared future in mind. A deposit on a house perhaps, a bit further down the line. The first cautious steps towards proper visible commitment. More than just that denoted by length of time.

Correction: what she'd *thought* was their shared future in mind.

Turned out putting in the hard work for Joe had been too much like…well, like hard work. Her heart froze again towards him, a cold hardening in her chest that made her throat contract and her eyes tingle.

She flashed a smile at the man walking next to her along the ornate galleried landing. Why not respond? What was there to stop her? It was so nice just to be found attractive – something that had been called into question deep inside her since she'd discovered Joe's betrayal.

It hadn't helped that she'd discovered the full horror of Joe's infidelity after a particularly long hard day working on the McNulty garden. There had been soil in her unkempt hair, dirt under her fingernails and across one cheek, and Joe hadn't missed the chance to build his defence on exactly that. Then again, did she think she might somehow have felt better about him playing away if she'd been dressed up to the nines with her hair and make-up done? *Idiot.* She was too work-obsessed, he'd said, she never made any effort to look good for him anymore, she'd stopped being fun. All comments designed to make him feel better about his behaviour by making her feel worse.

Human nature. That didn't stop it from hurting.

And so a bit of harmless attention from a man who looked like an off-duty aftershave model with his open-necked white shirt, perfect suit, tousled hair and lop-sided smile was just the thing to kick off the Make-Izzy-Strong Reinvention Mini-Break.

'I'm this way,' she smiled at him, coming to a stop and tilting her chin at the sign on the wall listing room numbers. He inclined his head almost imperceptibly, the hazel eyes holding her own for just a beat too long. Her stomach, now awakened, wasn't about to quit and gave a slow and delicious flip.

'Oliver Forbes,' he said, holding out his right hand. Easy for him, he had minimal luggage.

She looked from his hand to his face. The smile was still there. She shifted her case from one hand to the other and shook hands briefly with him.

'Izzy,' she said. 'Thanks again for before.'

Oliver Forbes watched from the corner of his eye as she held her head high and lugged her own bags down the passage, key card poised in her hand.

Her unease in the lobby had been almost palpable, drawing in his attention until the rest of the bustle around him seemed to pale into the background. Her finger-drumming impatience at the bureaucracies of check-in, the blush of embarrassment as she cleared up after knocking the plant flying that managed to highlight her porcelain skin so prettily. She was clearly desperate to escape to her room.

He wasn't usually given to noticing such detail.

Then again, he'd been knocked off-centre by the tedium of taking a hotel stay when what he'd wanted, what he'd *expected* was the work to have been finished on his new house in Highgate by the moment he *chose* to move into it. Turned out his travel and business commitments had lulled his supposedly impeccable team of contractors into a false sense of security over the urgency of the work. Not good enough. Heads would roll.

In the meantime, since he faced a few more days without his private refuge, a face like hers with its blush touching the smooth cheekbones and its tiny spray of golden freckles on her nose, was a welcome distraction.

Gardener? Really?

He took in her appearance as she walked away. Softly curving figure, long legs, healthy-looking rather than skinny. Honey coloured hair gathered loosely at the nape of her neck, touched gold at the ends by the sun. Lightly sun-kissed cheeks and nose beneath minimal make-up. No jewellery, no nail varnish, no accessories. Suddenly her stated profession seemed more plausible.

He wondered what she was doing, checking in alone to her booking for two. He'd barely registered anything his own receptionist had said, it had been far more interesting to listen to Izzy's discomfort at check-in. Damsels in Distress – his particular weakness.

Because where there was fluster, there was always a way in.

***

Izzy slid the door key card into the slot and pushed the panelled door open, still enjoying the afterglow of his attention. The smile on her face faded on her lips as she leaned back against the closing door and drew in a long breath.

'Oh hell,' she muttered out loud.

So the Spa Treatment wasn't an end to it. In the course of the joint brainwave with her friends to turn the intended surprise night away with Joe into a Get-Over-Him Mini-Break for herself, she had failed to remember that she'd booked the hotel's Romantic Getaway Package for two.

It wasn't called that for nothing.

Was there anything in this room that wasn't his-and-hers? Her eyes took in matching white fluffy bathrobes and waffle slippers, two crystal flutes stood next to the complimentary champagne. And as she walked into the adjoining bathroom she was greeted by Jack-n-Jill sinks.

She stared at her own dismayed face in the ornate scrolled

mirror above them. How the hell was she meant to stop thinking about Joe when this whole place was a made-for-two luxury nightmare that mocked her from every angle?

CHAPTER 2

IZZY SHAW'S GET-OVER-THE-BASTARD ACTION LIST

1) Enlist friends for supportive esteem-building summit meetings.
2) Stock up on wine and ice cream and eat/drink without regard for calorie counting.
3) Calculate budget for Joe's intended birthday and Christmas gifts and spend said amount on treating self to new clothes.
4) eBay his collection of football programmes and add profit to own treat-budget.
5) Make list of all Joe's faults for reference at weak moments.
6) Block him on Facebook and delete all texts and messages from him before responding.
7) Book up girls' nights out for the next couple of months.
8) Take a night away for me-time, pampering and contemplation.
9) Don't get even, get even better. Have a no-strings one night stand.

Izzy leaned back against the smooth tiled wall and closed her eyes to soak up every ounce of relaxation that hot steam had to offer. Tension in her shoulders ingrained from the endless bending and stretching that came with her job slowly began to loosen its grip. It was early evening now and she had the basement pool area and steam room almost to herself as people drifted away to get ready to go out or have dinner. No rush for that. Her appetite hadn't been up to much these last few weeks, she'd rather stay here a bit longer.

When door opened and Oliver Forbes climbed into the steam room, she took an unintentional deep breath, filling her lungs with steam and launching a spectacular coughing fit.

He stared at her through the hot mist, one hand on the door.

'Are you OK?' he asked doubtfully.

She turned away, her eyes and nose streaming, one hand plastered over her mouth, the other flapping at him.

'Fine,' she croaked in between hacking.

He sat down on the opposite bench and raised one foot. As she gradually got her cough under control she was grateful for the steam, which she hoped might hide her undoubtedly tomato-red face.

She offered his concerned expression an I'm-perfectly-alright smile and he nodded and closed his eyes, leaning his head back against the tiles. Hah! The perfect opportunity to steal a proper sneaky look at him in his dark blue swim shorts. He had the most toned abs she'd ever seen. Broad shoulders, lean and fit body, legs roped with muscle. His dark hair was damply tousled from the steam and he had a light tan. She imagined him on some extreme sports holiday abroad, leaping off a cliff in the sunshine.

He opened his eyes unexpectedly and she snapped her gaze away and examined her fingernails.

'How's the stay going?' he asked. 'Making good use of the spa?'

She knew just from his pointed tone of voice and the smile that lurked on his lips that he'd overheard at check-in.

'Trying to,' she said. 'It's all such a treat, especially the whirlpool bath and steam room. I get a lot of back pain in my job.'

She raised eyebrows at his cheeky grin.

'What now?'

'I was imagining you with a shovel.'

'What can I say, I give good garden,' she said. 'What about you? Are you here for the leisure complex too?'

'Not really,' he said. 'Not that the gym and spa aren't a nice bonus. This is a bit of an unscheduled stay. It's in a good location for me for work.'

'How long are you staying?'

He shrugged.

'As long as I need to.'

So he was clearly not on the budget break. Why was she even surprised? Everything about him oozed cash – the clothes he'd worn at check-in, the expensive leather overnight bag, the way he spoke.

'You?' he asked.

'It's a treat break,' she said. 'You know, one of those packages you can book. Dinner, bed and breakfast with use of the spa thrown in.'

He was looking at her politely and she supposed he'd never had to look for the deal price in his life.

'So just the one night, 'she added.

'Better make it count, then,' he said and the way he held her eyes a moment too long made it feel like he wasn't just talking about the spa and the gourmet restaurant. Her stomach felt suddenly melty, not helped by the fact she was hitting the edge of her heat tolerance.

'I am,' she said. 'I've tried out every facility in the spa, well, the free ones anyway, and I've still got dinner to go. Then tomorrow I hit the shops.' She stood up. 'I need to cool down. Excuse me.'

She stood eyes closed under the aromatherapy shower, letting it cool her skin, then walked around the pool to the lounger where she'd left her bag and towel. Oliver Forbes with his perfect body was still in the steam room. Instead of lying back on the towel she picked it up and automatically wrapped it around her. Confidence in the way she looked wasn't her strong point right now. If Joe was washed up drowning on a beach she'd throw a bucket of water over him, but that didn't diminish the little seeds of doubt he'd planted in her mind when he'd tried to shift some of the blame for his behaviour her way. OK so she knew she was carrying a few extra pounds, mainly around the hips, but she'd been so sure of Joe's love she hadn't given it a second thought before.

Oliver Forbes emerged from the steam room and stood under the shower. She watched as the water cascaded over his body, knowing she shouldn't be staring but unable to tear her eyes away. Joe hadn't been keen on exercise beyond playing a bit of football with his mates. What might it feel like to be with someone that fit? He grabbed a towel from a row of hooks, then skirted the pool and headed towards her.

'You mind?' he indicated the lounger next to her. There was a roomful of them to choose from and he wanted that one? Her heart gave a tiny skip.

She shrugged and he sat down, rubbing his hair with a corner of the towel.

'Drink?' he asked, reaching for the phone on the table between loungers.

She looked up at him. A drink? A flurry of excited butterflies zipped briefly through her stomach before common sense bashed them into submission. A drink did *not* mean he was hitting on her, and even if he was she couldn't be less interested. Someone like him would never look twice at her, he was obviously just being polite.

Her own package deal danced through her mind. Outside its remit, you were practically charged for drawing breath in this place. Why not take him up on the drink, it meant nothing.

'I'd love coffee,' she said.

He gave the order over the phone and sat back.

'I can't remember the last time I went swimming,' she said, pulling her own towel a little closer around her.

'You don't belong to a gym?'

That meant he did, presumably. Who was she kidding, of course he did. You didn't get abs like that from sitting around watching TV. He clearly put in a lot of work.

She shook her head.

'My working hours are long,' she said. 'Sometimes I'm so tired by the time I get home the last thing I'd want to do is more exercise.'

'I thought your job was more about potting plants,' he said, a grin touching his lips. 'I didn't realise it could be so physically demanding.'

She raised an eyebrow.

'It's not standing with a basket picking flowers,' she said. 'There's a lot of heavy work involved. You have to be prepared to get your hands dirty.'

He reached across suddenly and paused, hand outstretched. 'May I?'

She stared. What exactly was he playing at?

She watched in surprise as he took one of her hands in his, no impulse kicked in to pull it away despite the sudden hot feeling in her stomach. He uncurled her fingers to see the palm and turned her hand to see her fingernails.

'This doesn't look like the hand of a heavyweight gardener,' he said.

She took her hand away and held both of them up.

'Yeah well, it's amazing what a bit of hand cream can do. Sometimes at the end of a working day they look like shovels.'

'So gym, spa treatments and swimming is a welcome break then. Is this something you do often?'

Because she really *looked* like a gym bunny. Not.

'Not often. I'm treating myself.'

'And you prefer to do that alone?'

Her self-consciousness about staying here alone resurfaced and she squashed it back down.

'It wasn't supposed to be a solitary thing,' she said.

'No?'

For a moment she considered fobbing him off, but she was used to being the subject of gossip now. Why bother making up some story for someone she didn't know and didn't care about?

'I booked the room for a romantic night away with my boyfriend.' She looked him boldly in the eye. Nothing to be embarrassed about. 'This hotel offers themed breaks – dinner, spa, breakfast, one price and it's all included. Ex-boyfriend now,' she added, pasting on an I-couldn't-care-less smile, to prove she was absolutely fine with that.

'You came alone on your own romantic night away?' He sounded amused. 'You didn't cancel?'

She couldn't blame him. It did sound a bit insane spoken out loud. She squared her shoulders.

'It seemed a shame to waste it,' she said. 'It was a non-refundable payment. So I figured I'd turn it into a Reinvention Break instead.'

She mumbled the last part and he leaned in close enough for her to see the tiny droplets of water that still clung to his skin and hair. A light frown touched his eyebrows.

'Reinvention? Of what?'

She looked straight at him. He was a total stranger, what the hell did she care what he thought?

'Of me,' she said.

Oliver leaned back in his lounger as their coffee arrived, watching her, all obstinate bravado protesting that she didn't care.

'Odd choice of word, 'reinvention'', he said, when the waiter had gone. 'Implies that you need to change. Which in turn implies that you're somehow responsible for whatever went wrong.'

'I'm not!' she snapped.

He looked at her over his coffee cup.

'Call it something else then. Not reinvention. I haven't seen anything about you yet that I'd change.'

As he heard her light intake of breath and saw a touch of blush rise high on her cheekbones, he wondered when she'd last received a compliment. *Long-term complacent relationship? A breeding ground for lack of appreciation.* All he had to do was take advantage of that.

There was something very appealing about her at close quarters. Put aside for a moment the fact that she was pretty, albeit in a dishevelled outdoorsy sort of way. There was an air of defiance about her that he liked. Whatever the ex-boyfriend had done, she wasn't sitting at home crying into her pillow was she? She'd kicked him into touch and had turned her romantic break into a treat. He couldn't help but admire that fighting spirit.

'How about I call it my Freedom Break instead then,' she said. 'Shopping and spa relaxation. Just what I need.'

'Perfect,' he said. 'And tonight?'

He held her gaze intently with his own. She didn't drop her eyes. Encouraging.

'A luxury meal in the restaurant,' she said.

'Alone?'

'I'm quite happy with my own company.'

'Understandable.' He paused, then added in another compliment. 'I like it too.' He paused to gauge the effect and when she smiled softly he zoomed in.

'How about having dinner with me? The place is full of couples. We can keep each other company.'

There was a sudden loud clatter as she dropped her cup into the saucer from a height and then tried to cover up her mistake by fiddling with the spoon. He watched, enjoying putting her on edge.

'Don't you have some kind of other plans?' she said, not looking up, furiously stirring the remains of her coffee.

He leaned back against the lounger and took a sip of his own drink.

'Nope. Dinner alone for me too. And I'd much prefer your company to my own.' He waited and then added in extra encouragement . 'It would be my treat of course.' He paused. 'Unless you want some time alone to – you know – get over things.'

That finally seemed to galvanise her into action. The implication that she was here to lick her wounds, that she might spend the evening crying into her pillow and enjoying the martyrdom of sitting alone in the sumptuous restaurant among the loved-up couples.

She put her coffee cup down on the table, no clatter this time, and sat back taking in the surroundings. A pause this long was not a good sign. *Win some, lose some.* Not that he ever lost out on a dinner date, or more, when he put his mind to it. For some reason the thought of missing out on this one brought a disappointed stab in his chest. Must be the thought of being stuck here overnight with no entertainment when he should be settling into his newly-finished luxury pad.

Then she looked at him, a tiny smile playing about her full lips, and his heart turned over softly.

'Dinner is thrown into my booking,' she said. 'It's a package deal. Spa treatments, dinner, bed and breakfast. So maybe *you'd* like to have dinner with *me*?'

He stared at her, momentarily wrong-footed. Had she really just counter-offered him on dinner? There was a hint of challenge in her eyes that made his mouth leech of moisture, as if he'd sunk his teeth into one of the hotel's fluffy towels.

'Sod the thrown-in dinner,' he said. 'You'll get the package-deal dinner menu, nothing worth having. Have dinner with me and choose what you like.'

***

Izzy pawed through the contents of her overnight bag and laid out the only possibility on the bed.

If she'd known she'd be having dinner with male model material, she would have packed something a bit more alluring than the maxi skirt, top and cardigan. She'd planned on eating early to avoid any pitying stares, followed by a likely return to the spa with a stack of magazines. At least she'd packed matching underwear instead of any greying old cotton.

Not that her underwear should matter. Because this was just dinner – right?

She looked at her reflection in the scroll-edged upright mirror. Her hair had behaved itself for once, the unruly waves lying softly over one shoulder.

Did she really think a man like him, on his own for the night in a luxury hotel, would ask a girl he didn't know to dinner with nothing more in mind than eating a meal? Her stomach gave a slow and delicious flip at the thought and she pressed her hands hard against it to make it stop. Rubbish. Why the hell was she reading any more into it than just dinner? And wasn't it irrelevant anyway? What mattered was the alternative – sitting alone in the restaurant at a table for two surrounded by couples playing footsie.

Whether he expected something in return or not, she didn't have to give it. She could have dinner with him, enjoy an evening of flirting and then walk away with her self-esteem happily boosted.

Unless she wanted more.

Item nine on her GET-OVER-THE-BASTARD LIST pranced through her mind. *Don't get even, get even better...*

She sat down hard on the bed. Where had that come from? By the time they reached the end of compiling the list, she and Shauna had been pretty drunk. A one-night-stand had been added as more of a laugh than anything, because of course they both knew that Izzy Shaw didn't *do* that kind of thing.

She shook her head lightly to clear it. Dinner didn't have to lead anywhere. She was safe, dependable play-by-the-rules Izzy. Impetuous flings with strangers were not part of that remit.

Because of course that remit had really worked for her in the past. *Not.*

The fluttering in her stomach was back with a vengeance.

***

A tiny heart-shaped chocolate made up the centrepiece of each place setting in the candlelit dining room, soft piano played in the background and the set menu was a special romance-themed selection.

Oliver stared at the pink embossed menu, eyebrows raised.

'Romantic Getaway Three Course Menu For Two...' he read.

Her cheeks felt a little too warm and she didn't look up. Instead she picked up her heart-shaped chocolate and dropped it into her purse. After a pause, she added his chocolate too. With no need to diet ever again, she could scoff them at leisure.

'Like I said, it's a package deal break. Dinner, bed and breakfast for one all-in price.'

Oliver beckoned the waiter and issued swift orders for a bottle of champagne and the standard menu while she tried to control the mad squiggling in her stomach.

'Like *I* said, sod the knocked-down package break.' The waiter returned and handed her the full restaurant menu. 'Choose whatever you like.'

***

Oliver watched her as she tucked into the main course of roasted sea bass with celeriac and truffle with obvious enjoyment. She'd finished every bite of the starter, too. He liked her uninhibited delight in the food. And he liked her relaxed outfit. She wore her hair loose, and just a touch of makeup highlighted the grey-green eyes and long eyelashes. Her lips looked peachily softer than ever with a touch of gloss. He was used to high maintenance – glossy, manicured women who picked at their food and obsessed about their appearance. So used to it in fact that it had become the norm. Being with her was like eating a sharp sorbet after a very cloying main meal.

'You said this place is convenient for work,' she said, between mouthfuls. 'What is it that you do?'

'I'm a lawyer,' he said. 'I travel a lot, but I'm based in London. This hotel is close to my office.'

She frowned.

'Why the need for a hotel then, if you live in the city? Don't you keep a house here?'

He thought of his beautiful new house, supposed to be finished a week ago to a stunningly high spec. His irritation at the delay seemed to have dissipated a little in her company.

'I have a house, bought it a few months ago, in Highgate.'

He didn't miss the brief widening of her eyes. Highgate was one of the most exclusive and beautiful suburbs of the city.

'Lucky you,' she said.

'I would be, if I could move into the damn place,' he said.

'What do you mean?'

'It's been gutted and refurbished from scratch,' he said. 'The whole thing needed stripping back. So redecorating, floors laid, kitchen and bathroom installation, everything. I've been away because of work so I've missed the worst of the disruption. It was meant to be finished a week ago. That's why I'm staying here, because my building team have overrun.'

'Do you have a project manager?'

He shook his head.

'I'm in control of it myself.'

'That's why it's overrun then,' she said. 'It would be like me handing over the plans for a garden and just letting the project cruise along rudderless. Things just don't get done sometimes if you're not there to kick butt.'

The implication that the delay was down to him irked a little and he made himself ignore it. To be fair, she had a point. He might have total focused control over his work but leaving things to chance in any other area of his life was clearly also a bad move.

'It should be finished in a day or two,' he said. 'And it'll be great to have somewhere to stay that feels like home,' he said. 'When I'm in London at least.'

'So you stay in hotels a lot then. For work?'

He thought he picked up a slight edge to her tone, but her face hadn't changed.

He nodded.

'I'm pretty good at living out of a suitcase. After a while it becomes second nature, luggage gets pared down, you start to use the same places in the same cities. It gets to be a way of life.'

'Doesn't it get lonely, being away like that?'

Something in that sentence touched him, and he paused for a moment to sip his drink and rationalise it. Loneliness was just a word. It meant focus and drive. It was a positive not a negative if you wanted success. And he could always find company if he wanted it, a non-committal brief encounter was easy to come by on the international hotel circuit.

'It helps if you like your own company,' he said. 'Sometimes you come across the same work contacts. It varies. Sometimes you meet new people. It doesn't have to be isolated if you don't want it to be.'

She sat back a little in her seat, her gaze holding his, a hint of knowing in the grey-green eyes that he couldn't fathom.

'Like tonight, you mean. Like me.'

He nodded.

'Yes. Room service or dinner with you. No contest.'

Her posture stiffened almost imperceptibly, as if some thought had occurred to her. The gaze didn't waver and she tilted her chin as she looked at him, an almost judgemental look in her eyes. Then she looked down at her champagne flute and the moment was gone.

Izzy took a sip of her champagne. Serial hotel guest... lots of travel for work...doesn't have to be isolated if you don't want it to be.

She pushed her plate to one side.

Don't get even. Get even better...

Curiosity needled at her. Hotels, girls, one-night-stands. Was this the way Joe had behaved when he was away supposedly working towards their future? Did he single out the best prospect and ask her to dinner? Was that how it had started? Was she seeing that dark mirror image of her own life?

She wanted, *needed* to see more. This had nothing to do with revenge, this was about understanding. For the first time she had a flash of the type of woman who inhabited Joe's alternative fun life, that foil to herself – the type of woman who held things together at home. An image of her mother flashed unbidden into her mind, the person she'd vowed never to become. Fifties cupcake housewife living in the wrong decade. Izzy might have bucked that trend with her traditionally male-dominated work, but she'd fallen right into the same trap in her relationship.

This was her chance. Her opportunity to flout the rules and be the other woman for once instead of the homemaker. Exactly what *was* the fun she was missing out on? Her heart picked up speed in anticipation of where this thought process might lead.

'It must be difficult to keep a relationship going when you're travelling a lot,' she said, keeping her voice carefully neutral.

Oliver finished his main course and pushed the plate to one side.

'I imagine it would be,' he said. 'I don't do them.'

She stared at him.

'Not at all?'

'Not in the long-term sense.' He took a sip of his drink. 'My work comes first, it always has. I need that focus and I can never predict the hours I'll be working or where I'll need to be. It wouldn't be fair to drag another person along on that ride.'

Nothing detracted from the need for irreversible success, that aim which never quite felt within reach. Allowing a relationship to distract him from work would be unheard of, would go against every instinct he'd learned growing up.

'Relationships are not all they are cracked up to be,' he said.

She gave a rueful laugh.

'I'll drink to that.' She raised her drink and he nodded and picked his own glass up in response.

'Relationships, relationships,' he said. 'All that grief, all that input.'

'It's not a one-way street,' she said. 'You're meant to get something back.'

'Doesn't sound like *you* did,' he countered, but she didn't reply, just met his gaze with her grey-green eyes.

'Relationships sap the energy from what can be a perfect meeting of the physical,' he said.

He watched carefully for her response to that and noticed her shift almost imperceptibly in her seat.

'You mean a fling.'

He shrugged.

'If you want to call it that. It's perfectly simple. You've obviously been messed around by some idiot who's treated you badly. Doesn't sound remotely like fun to me. The way I play it, things never get beyond the fun stage. You never discover the loathsome habits. You never even make it to your first argument. I don't have time to deal with any of that.'

'You don't even date?' she clarified.

He shook his head.

'Why let things get that far?'

A tiny smile touched the corner of her mouth and his pulse began to climb.

'That's very interesting,' she said.

'Is it?'

She toyed with her glass. As he watched the slender fingers slowly and rhythmically turning the stem of it, heat began to tingle low in his abdomen.

'I'd be lying if I said I haven't been feeling a bit low,' she said. 'The break up came out of the blue, smacked me between the eyes.' She looked up. 'It's all fine though, I have a planned strategy.' She gave him another smile.

'Dinner with a stranger part of that strategy?' he said.

'Not dinner exactly,' she said, and he saw a flash of something in her eyes.

'What then?'

She blushed prettily and took a sip of her drink. Saying nothing said it all and he zoomed in immediately. Knowing when to pounce was key.

'Ah, I see.'

'Do you?' She looked up at him, eyes slightly narrowed.

He held her gaze.

'No better way to draw a line under a break-up,' he said. 'What you need now is concrete approval from someone with no agenda that you're beautiful and appealing and sexy. Which, by the way, you are. All those things you've been secretly questioning about yourself.'

The suggestion, oblique, not direct, was clear enough that he might as well have announced it to the restaurant. Izzy's heart thundered in her chest so fast she could hear it in her ears. Every nerve sparked with excitement, heat tingled between her legs, she felt more alive than she could remember.

A couple of hours in the company of Oliver Forbes and she felt like she could conquer the world.

How might you feel after the night with him? Her mind whispered, and a rippling shiver sparkled the length of her spine. She met the hazel eyes, holding herself steady despite her shortening breath.

'Don't you ever feel like being reckless?' he said.

She saw the heat inherent in his eyes and instead of feeling wary, she felt unexpectedly inspired. Whatever his motivation was, it had no relevance to her. She could make this situation whatever she wanted it to be. When had she ever done anything for the pure fun and pleasure of it, without analysing the hell out of it first? When had she last lived in the moment?

You couldn't get much more living-in-the-moment than a no-strings one-night-stand.

Dessert arrived. A delectable pot of creamy lemon posset with raspberry running through it that she really didn't want and that neither of them ate.

Oliver beckoned the waiter.

'Would you like coffee?' he asked them.

She looked Oliver straight in the eye.
'Why don't we have coffee upstairs?' she said.

CHAPTER 3

She was acutely aware of his hand at the small of her back as he accompanied her through the velvet and marble of the lobby and up the sweeping staircase. At the top of the stairs next to the sign where they'd parted after check-in, she paused.

Still time to back out.

Izzy Shaw didn't do reckless and impulsive. She did spot-on timekeeping, she did savings accounts, she gave bloody good girlfriend.

The soft fluttering of excitement in her stomach was tempered by a vague feeling that this was somehow wrong. She clamped down hard on that thought. How could it be wrong? Just who or what was she being unfaithful to here? Some stupid idealised future that she'd been so committed to she couldn't see what was going on under her nose? She shoved all thoughts of unfaithfulness away. She was free and single and she could do as she chose.

'Your place or mine?' he said.

The last stop before she left sensible Izzy outside the bedroom door. Common sense kicked in with a list of considerations. Her friends knew her room number, her phone and her belongings were in there and she knew for a fact there were condoms lurking in the zip pocket of her case, left over from a long ago weekend away she'd spent with Joe.

'Mine,' she said.

At the door she paused to look up at him in the soft light from the hallway. Nerves were there, of course they were, sharpening her senses to a needle point. But alongside them was desire to break out of the mould she was in. And more. As he locked eyes with her, his hand circling the base of her spine generating sparks of promise, she was shocked by the strength of her physical desire for him.

She could hear her heartbeat in her ears. The moment they were inside the room she closed the door behind her. All the romance of the made-for-two suite stood beyond, the bed now turned down and pink tissue paper-wrapped chocolates on the his 'n' hers fluffy pillows.

Was she really going to do this? Sleep with someone she'd only just met?

Never in a million years would she have picked someone up in a bar and had a one-night-stand. The whole situation she was in lent itself to this, as if it was somehow meant to be. The anonymity of the hotel room, the fact he had no idea beyond her first name and a bit of background who the hell she was. No knowledge of her hangups, her failings, her aspirations, her past or future. It was like existing in a bubble. The inherent danger of what she was doing seemed far away – her friends knew where she was, she hadn't gone back to his place, he'd told her he was a lawyer and she had no reason to disbelieve him. The only thing stopping her was the idea that this was out of character or somehow wrong.

To hell with that.

If Joe could do it, then so could she.

And that was why she'd let things get this far. Why she wasn't stopping things in their tracks. Because a one-night-stand was the perfect antidote to the poison Joe had tainted her with. No strings. One night of therapy. Call it payback. Call it an ego boost. Call it what you like. She couldn't conceive right now of trusting another man with the intricacies of her life. She had no need for a man she could turn to or rely on only to have her hopes crushed somewhere down the line. She needed some fun, and he was perfect for that because the type of man who went in for one-night-stands was exactly the type of man she would never give life-space to again.

Why not taste the other side just this once. Being reliable, loving Izzy had got her zilch. Less than zilch in fact. A broken heart.

Before she could lose her nerve, she turned towards him, stood on tiptoe and touched his lips briefly with her own, registering his surprised intake of breath and relishing it.

His hand moved to caress her jaw as she looked up into his eyes. Clear hazel, speckled with yellow. She breathed in the faint spice of aftershave on warm skin. He took control, tilted her chin gently and kissed her, softly at first and then with growing hunger, his fingers tangling in her hair, his free hand sliding around her waist. She could taste the faint twist of red wine from dinner on his lips.

She felt light headed, and as the last tendrils of sensibility began to slip away she made herself break the kiss. She took a couple of calming breaths, her hands on his chest, sharply aware of his hands circling her back and the hardness of his body against hers.

'Ground rules,' she managed, trying not to pant.

He gave her a look of intensity and amusement.

'Ground rules?' he said. A smile touched the corner of his mouth. 'When you say ground rules maybe you mean second thoughts.'

She shook her head immediately.

Out-of-character was intoxicating in a way she had never imagined. She was sweet, dependable, hardworking, loyal Izzy.

Joe's Doormat.

In this room she could be none of these things, especially that last one. Oliver would know her as whatever she wanted to be. The excitement that thought invoked made her stomach flutter deliciously and she was glad of his arms around her because her knees felt suddenly like they might fold underneath her.

'No second thoughts,' she said. 'Ground rules.'

She waited until he nodded.

'This is a one-off. No strings, no comeback. No follow-up date, no swapping phone numbers, no poking me on Facebook. This is a one-night-only take-it-or-leave-it experience. Agreed?'

He looked into her grey-green eyes, at the bold, defensive expression in them. She was utterly adorable. He felt an absurd desire to press rewind just so he could be sure he'd heard her correctly. The novelty of being on the receiving end of the proposition wrong-footed him. Of course he'd read the signals, would have made a move himself if she hadn't kissed him like that. He had nothing to lose, this being the usual deal.

Except that she'd turned out not to be the usual deal. She had her own agenda.

Miss Sensible Garden Expert. Maybe this was her getting back at her boyfriend, whatever he'd done. A one-night-stand to make her feel better. Whatever it was, he blocked consideration of it from his mind. Why make this more than it needed to be? No strings suited him down to the ground, a fling was the only kind of relationship he indulged in. Yet he'd never had a girl set the tone from the outset before.

He was used to driving the situation, making his intentions clear, distancing himself afterwards. To have her take that role was an enticing novelty and it flamed his desire for her on a visceral level that made him want to scoop her up and take her right now, no preamble. Instead he made himself go slowly, sensing there was fragility beneath her bravado. He could tell by the way she trembled under his hands that she was out of her comfort zone, however determined she might be not to show it.

'Agreed,' he said and stopped her mouth with another kiss. Deeper this time, a chance to feel and taste.

Decision made now. Stupid misplaced guilt shoved away. This was her time, the ultimate indulgence. She could take from him whatever she wanted with no fear of comeback afterwards. She could use him however she wanted to.

Tentatively, slowly at first, nerves competing with desire in her fluttering stomach, she let her curiosity take over, let her hands go where they wanted. His hand moved to caress her cheek and slide behind her head, tilting her face to the perfect angle. He had caught the curve of her lips perfectly in his, easing them apart and caressing with his tongue, sending waves of heat through her body to tingle between her legs. His other hand traced her spine and cupped the curve of her bottom to press her against him, melding her body hard against his so she could feel his growing arousal.

In the slide of her hands up his chest she could feel hard muscle beneath his shirt, and she moved fingers to buttons, tugging them open until she could slide greedy hands beneath, across the warm taut contours of his chest. She eased his shirt off and dropped it on the floor. How different he felt. He was much broader than Joe and far more toned. Three years with the same man and the very newness of this sparked her hunger for him even further.

In one shrug her sparkly cardigan fell from her shoulders to the floor. She gasped against his mouth as he kept her hard against him with one hand and slipped the other from her hair, across tingling skin to pull the straps of her camisole from her bare shoulders. He traced his lips from her mouth slowly down her neck in a trail of tiny soft kisses, making her writhe as he reached the hollow spot above her collarbones. Her top slipped down into a silky pool around her waist. Instead of undoing her bra, he eased the cups down to gently reveal and push up her breasts, the hard buds of her nipples now exposed for the taking as he slid his mouth lower still. She sucked in a sharp breath as he closed his lips over a nipple and stroked its tip gently with his tongue, sending dizzying waves through her right down to her toes.

The knowledge that this was a one-off unleashed inhibitions so ingrained she'd thought them unshakeable, had assumed they were simply part of her. Her hang ups about her appearance were shoved to one side. Who cared that she'd never gotten around to losing that extra couple of pounds from her thighs? Why would it matter if she made some move that might shock, if she took the lead? Sex with Joe had been shrouded by a duvet, had been horizontal, even way back when they'd first met. Unimaginative beyond what he assumed did it for them, she never indicated otherwise, not wanting to hurt his feelings, satisfied enough with her assumption that this was how it was between two people. She had enjoyed it, the intimacy of it, the sensation of it, but it had never blown her away. No, it had never done that.

She had no one here to please save herself. No need to worry about hurting Oliver's feelings because she didn't know him, didn't care about him, no need to worry about shocking him because she'd never see him again after this. When had she ever felt this free? So eager to take all the pleasure she could get?

Smoothing her hands over his taut abdomen, she let them go lower, eager now to explore every inch of him. She tugged at his belt until it came free and waited for him to step out of his clothes. Her own maxi skirt fell softly into a puddle at her feet. She stroked her hands softly over the length of his erection, testing the texture, the size, the feel of him with tentative fingertips. His sharp intake of breath in response to her touch thrilled her.

I did that.

She eased her stroking into a slow, deliberate rhythm, feeling him react in the hiss of his breath against her neck and the tension of his body, loving the way she could evoke a response. Feeling desirable for once, knowing he wanted her and that she was toying with that want, she felt deliciously empowered.

Gently seizing control back, he curled his hands beneath her and lifted her gently, her hard nipples grazing his chest, her legs hooked behind his waist. His mouth slid back against hers with more passion now as he crossed the room and lowered her gently back onto the softness of the huge bed.

The sheet was cool and smooth against her back and his mouth was back against hers, his hands removing her bra, tugging her top off and casting it aside, exploring her body. Her mind followed the progress of his fingers downwards, anticipation rising as he caressed her softly through the damp lace of her panties. Teasing, circular motions that made her ache for him to go further. Her breath hitched against his lips as he eased her panties down and away and then he was stroking his way up her inner thighs until his fingertips teased featherlight strokes over her most sensitive place. Hot desire flooded her, pushing everything else out of her consciousness as she squirmed to cover his hand with her own, wanting his fingers inside her, wanting more than that. He refused to be rushed, simply took her hand away and held it lightly in his free hand as he continued to circle the nub of her with his thumb, making her wait until she was dizzy with need, all other thoughts gone from her mind. Then he slid two fingers inside her all the way. She cried out as he moved them in a slow rhythm, his thumb still stroking, the delicious friction driving her to heights of pleasure she hadn't known existed.

As she regained control bit by bit, he tugged gently at her hip until he'd turned her over. The sheet felt momentarily cool against her stomach and breasts and then he slid his hands to the front of her thighs and pulled her back against him until she was on her knees. A pause as he ripped open a condom and then she felt his erection, big and hard between her thighs. She bit her lip in anticipation as he rubbed it against her slick entrance and then he thrust smoothly forward, as far as he could go, deep inside her. She heard herself cry out softly and then he pulled back with smooth, tantalising slowness almost all the way, and began to thrust forward deeply again and again at a slow delicious pace. Her pleasure began to climb again.

Tangling a hand gently in her hair he tugged softly.

'Look,' he whispered. 'Look how gorgeous you are.'

She lifted her head, unsure of what he wanted, and then saw. The huge gilt mirror leaned against the opposite wall, depicting them in the honeyed glow of the single table lamp as he took her steadily from behind. He held her reflected gaze steadily with his own as he thrust into her again and again, one hand cupping her breast and teasing the nipple as the other moved between her legs to circle her most sensitive sweet spot with one finger. She moved against him, working towards the height of her pleasure, feeling it there for the taking, unable to tear her eyes away from the mirror, watching him take her. She felt the tension in his body change, his breathing up the pace, and as she finally tipped over into a sublime deliciousness she had never known he was right there with her.

***

The light filtering through Izzy's closed eyelids was brighter than she was used to, and her first thought was that she'd forgotten to shut the bedroom curtains in her flat.

She opened her eyes. The light was brighter because the high sash windows of the hotel room were dressed with the flimsiest of silk curtains. They put the tiny windows and concrete view of her flat to shame.

Boutique Hotel. Reinvention Get-Over-Joe Mini-Break. One-Night-Stand.

She froze in the king-size bed, the vague cushion of euphoria on which she had woken deflating as if stuck with a pin. She turned over inch by careful inch, knowing perfectly well what she would see before it came into view. She stuffed a mouthful of squashy pillow into her mouth to stifle her own squeak of shock.

Dark tousled hair, smooth skin with a faint tan, the beginnings of stubble on the chiselled jaw and thick eyelashes that were wasted on a guy. They'd spent half the night screwing every ounce of energy out of each other. Her toes curled just at the thought of it.

She peeled the pillow out of her mouth so she could take in a big calming breath.

It could be worse. Wasn't it practically obligatory for a one-night-stand to never look as good as you remembered them the next morning? He certainly bucked that trend. Which was more than could be said for her. Sitting up carefully, she caught sight of her own insane reflection in the huge gilt-framed mirror at the side of the room. Her hair stuck out at odd angles and last night's mascara was smudged panda-style beneath her eyes. Her face reddened as she flashed on last night's use of that mirror. Had that really been her? Shy, retiring Izzy?

She had to get out of here.

Thank goodness he was sound asleep. She checked her watch. A little past five o'clock. A new undiscovered benefit to having a body clock that woke you up at cockcrow no matter how little sleep you'd had: you could make a swift exit after an ill-conceived fling without discovery.

She held her breath and eased her way out of the bed then around the room, picking up her clothes, dressing, keeping every movement smooth and pin-drop quiet. Oliver didn't stir. She wondered randomly where in Highgate he lived, and squashed the thought immediately.

The flipside of last night's triumphant fingers-up at Joe trickled into her mind. Last night it had been all about getting even, all about trying to make some kind of sense of what he'd done so she might move on. Now in the cold light of morning the wider implications of what she'd done kicked in.

Was this what the morning after was like for Joe? Making a sharp exit, backing out of what he'd started before it went any further. She looked at the dark head on the pillow. All she knew of him was what he'd told her and she'd accepted it all without question. For the first time she saw a new parallel with Joe. Was there some other girl somewhere, thinking Oliver was away on a work trip, waiting for him to call her, trusting him? He'd told her he didn't do relationships, had sounded so convincing, but no doubt Joe said exactly the same thing to all his conquests.

She needed to get out of here. Right now, before he woke up.

CHAPTER 4

Oliver came to life slowly. Bright sunshine slanted onto the empty pillow next to him.

Not his hotel room. Not his bed. He leaned up on an elbow and rubbed his scratchy eyes. Not enough sleep.

The events of the previous night trickled back into his consciousness, driving out his usual first waking desire for caffeine, and he glanced immediately around the room.

For her.

No clothes anywhere. No cosmetics, no bags. No sign that he'd shared this room with anyone except for the crumpled bedclothes and the hot rerun that flashed into his mind. His stomach give a slow flip which he insisted to himself was due to hunger, nothing more. It was breakfast time, after all. He threw the covers back and checked the ensuite. There was no question about it – she was gone.

Unless.

Her package deal included dinner, bed and breakfast, didn't it? Maybe she'd decided to make the most of the thrown-in breakfast buffet on her way out. He dressed at speed and headed for the dining room, his shoes whispering on the deep nap of the carpet.

Not that he needed to see her this morning of course. All that needed to be said had been said the previous evening. They were both crystal clear about where they stood. It was simply a matter of politeness, right? Checking she was fine, saying a perfunctory goodbye before she checked out.

Down in the ornate dining room, no longer intimately candlelit and instead now flooded with sunlight from the high windows and reset for breakfast, he pointedly filled a glass with freshly squeezed orange juice from the buffet, while in reality he scanned the room for her.

Right up to the moment he realised she wasn't there he had been utterly certain that she would be. As his mood took a stupid inexplicable nosedive, he discarded the orange juice and left the room.

He approached the high marble desk in the morning-busy lobby poised to question the receptionist.

'Can I help you, Mr Forbes?' She remembered him from check-in yesterday. And he knew immediately from the over-attentive smile she gave him that with a few carefully-chosen sentences he could persuade her to give him the information he wanted. Izzy's last name might be a start.

He hesitated.

Ground rules, not second thoughts.

Her words of the previous night came back to him and he bit back the question that lurked in his mouth. If she'd wanted to be found she would have told him her name or left him a note. She would have joined him for breakfast. She wouldn't have made her excuses and left halfway through the night.

And why the hell was he feeling so piqued anyway? Just because she had robbed him of the chance to be in control, to be the one who did the backing-off?

He thought of the reason she'd been staying here. Some kind of waste-of-space boyfriend had let her down.

'Mr Forbes?'

'Can I order a newspaper?' he said randomly.

He took a breath.

What was he thinking? Like he needed or wanted a woman in

his life. Like he had time or headspace for that kind of distraction.

Let it go. Let her have got her own back for whatever wrong had been done to her. She'd done him a favour here, why the hell was he questioning it? One glorious night and he didn't even have the dirty work of backing out to do.

He realised suddenly that the receptionist had asked him three times which paper he would prefer.

Her quick exit should feel like a gift.

Why the hell then, had it left him feeling so short-changed?

***

'You had a one-night-stand?' Shauna stared at Izzy, incredulous. 'You?'

Izzy took a defensive sip of her coffee because she still couldn't quite believe her own behaviour, and glanced around the café to make sure no one had heard.

'It WAS on the 'Get-over-Him List,' she pointed out, keeping her voice low and hoping Shauna and Suzy might do the same. '*You* suggested it. Right there at number nine, right after eat your own body-weight in ice-cream, blow some cash on a new wardrobe and get plastered on white wine.' She paused. 'All of which I did.'

Shauna was shaking her head.

'It wasn't a *real* suggestion. I'd had a couple of drinks. It was just one of those things that come up when you brainstorm. I never for one second thought you'd actually DO that one. If I did, I would have told you about all the caveats that come with it.'

Oh for Pete's sake.

'Caveats?'

'Exactly.' Suzy, veteran reader of womens' magazines, leaned in as if about to impart a great secret. 'There are rules you need to follow if you're going to do something as reckless as have a one-night-stand.'

'Go on.'

37

She flapped a hand at Izzy, the other clapped to her forehead.

'Don't rush me, don't rush me, I'm trying to remember. OK, first and foremost, you don't pick anyone you're likely to encounter in daily life. Far too complicated. No bosses, no brother's-best-mates, no colleagues…'

'That's fine then,' Izzy said with a note of triumph. 'Box ticked.'

Suzy nodded approvingly. 'There's more.'

Of course there was.

'You make it clear from the outset there won't be anything further than this one night.'

Izzy took a sip of her coffee and nodded.

'Ground rules. I did all of that. I'm not a complete idiot.'

'Safe sex?' Shauna said and Izzy inhaled a mouthful of coffee.

'Of course,' she managed, trying not to cough.

'And you can give him no way of finding you afterwards. No phone number swapping.'

'Even if you want it to be more?' Izzy asked with sudden interest. Not, of course, that she did.

'*Especially* if you want it to be more. They never look that good the next morning you know. You go to sleep thinking you're with an Adonis and then you wake up and he looks like a troll.'

Whatever Izzy was uncertain of regarding the previous night, she was sure about one thing.

'He wasn't a troll,' she said. She could hardly think of him without her stomach melting.

'Trust me, he was. They always are. The magic never extends past the next morning,' Shauna insisted. 'Best to bail out of these things while it's all going well.' She sat back in her chair and folded her arms authoritatively. 'Basically, what it all comes down to is one thing: A one-night-stand can only ever be a success if it's anonymous. Meddle with that and it can only end badly.'

Suzy flapped a hand for Shauna to be quiet.

'Never mind all the rules. Did it WORK? That's the most impor-tant thing. Are you feeling better about what Joe did, are you empowered and ready to move on?'

A night with Oliver had certainly opened her eyes. It hadn't negated the loss but there was less of an ache somehow. She understood now that she hadn't so much been grieving for Joe but for the idealised future she'd had in her mind, which had included him. That had been her guiding light for over a year. Without it she'd felt like she was cruising round in circles. What she needed now was a sense of direction. And she intended to get that by throwing herself into her work, something that actually gave a return on the effort she put in.

As far as Joe was concerned, she was well out of it.

Being with Oliver had made her feel capable of that, better about herself. Made her feel like the gourmet meal instead of the usual boring old shepherd's pie. It had been the best fun she'd had in years.

She looked at Suzy and Shauna's expectant faces.

'Damn right I feel better for it,' she said. 'It was an ego boost.'

It was also over with.

She hadn't even told Oliver Forbes her last name. She'd never see him again.

She insisted to herself that was exactly what she wanted. There was no way in the real world she would want a man who thought nothing of having a one-night-stand with a woman he'd barely met. And let's not forget Oliver might have a girlfriend in the real world outside last night's bubble. Why the hell would she want to see him again? She may as well just call up Joe and invite him right back into her life.

Toe-curlingly gorgeous it might have been, but the one stomach-flipping night would have to be enough. Men were off-limits for the foreseeable future unless they happened to be offering her a big fat lucrative gardening contract.

***

Izzy pasted on another smile and shook yet another hand. Arabella and Gordon, her biggest clients to date, had been somehow landed through an advertisement she'd placed in the local paper and Izzy still couldn't quite believe they'd accepted her quote, even now the work was done. Thrilled to show off their newly-finished garden, they had thrown a summer party and true to their word had invited her along. She just wished she didn't feel quite so out of place. Perhaps if she'd worn her old jeans and work boots instead of the kitten heels and the silk tea dress that fluttered against her legs, she would have felt more like herself. She took a sip of champagne. It would all be worth it if she could pick up just one or two more contracts from this evening. Word of mouth was worth a hundred times more than newspaper ads. She'd put her heart and soul into this project and she was thrilled that Arabella and Gordon were so pleased with the result.

'And this is Gordon's solicitor,' Arabella said, tugging her by the arm as she struggled to digest all the new names and faces. She'd have to do some serious mingling after this if she was to make the most of the opportunity for new work, and nothing looked more unprofessional than getting someone's name wrong.

She turned, automatic bright smile pasted on her face, ready to meet as many people as Gordon and Arabella could throw at her, and her heart did an unbidden somersault as the smile gave way to stunned jaw-slackening.

It was him.

Last seen asleep in her bed as she made her quick exit from the Romantic Getaway suite. Six weeks had done a great job of convincing her he hadn't been all that, so the sight of him now - dark hair, perfect strong jaw, lopsided smile - sent her mind into a mad tailspin. His dark suit was impeccably cut, his tie was loosened and his shirt unbuttoned at the neck. He was utterly, breathtakingly gorgeous. She realised her mouth was hanging open and closed it with a snap.

'Oliver Forbes,' Arabella said. 'This is Izzy Shaw, our amazing project manager. Genius she is, never know it to look at her but she can wield a spade like a navvy.'

Warmth rose in Izzy's cheeks. For Pete's sake a more feminine introduction might have been nice.

He shook her hand, her fingers enveloped in his, the touch of him sparking dizzying flashbacks of the last time his skin had been against hers. Inhibitions, shed so easily when she knew she'd never see him again, flooded over her in a wash of icy shyness.

'Shaw?' he said, eyes fixed on hers, softly amused. Her face continued to burn.

'Isabella Shaw Garden Design', she managed.

Anonymity flew out of the window in that one sentence and she heard Shauna's voice in her head, *A no-strings-fling can only work if it's anonymous.* Formal introduction now precluded any repeat performance then. Good thing really, because from the bone-melting way he was looking at her, an encore obviously wasn't far from his mind. No chance of that now.

If you stick to the rules, a voice in her mind whispered. *If.* She crushed it. That voice belonged to another Izzy, one with a whole different and dangerous agenda that she thought she'd left behind in that hotel room.

'Would you both like another drink?' He didn't wait for a reply, just left them to cross the terrace to the drinks table and glasses of champagne, already poured for the taking.

'Gorgeous, isn't he,' Arabella said, linking her arm through Izzy's as they watched him. 'And such a lovely guy. Close friend of Gordon's, always happy to go the extra mile.'

'Really?'

It felt odd, listening to such basic character details about him when she already knew him so intimately on a physical level.

'Wasted of course. Never has a girlfriend, confirmed bachelor. Tried to introduce him to a couple of my single friends but he never shows an interest. Gordon says he's married to his work. But he's just renovated a new property and he might be in the market for garden remodelling if you play your cards right, darling.'

As Oliver made his way back and handed them each a glass, Arabella was mercifully oblivious that Izzy's knees had turned to jelly and she was concentrating hard on not swaying in her kitten heels.

'You should have seen the building site that was here before she turned up,' she told Oliver. 'The whole project ran like clockwork and we couldn't be more delighted. Do excuse me, both of you, lots more people arriving.'

Izzy deliberately focused on Arabella's back as she drifted away, freshening drinks and making small talk as she went. She felt his gaze upon her and held her champagne flute in a vice-grip to stop her fingers from shaking. *There was no wronged girlfriend.* No third person fallout to feel guilty about. Whatever their night together had been about for him, it wasn't playing away. His motives were not the same as Joe's. Guilt relinquished its grip on her and the memory of the deliciousness of their night together came crashing back to her, this time unfettered by it. Her mouth felt dust dry.

'I didn't think I'd see you again,' he said.

She took a fortifying sip of champagne to wet her lips and distract her fluttering stomach.

'You weren't meant to,' she said. 'That was the whole point of having ground rules.'

'Ah yes, the ground rules,' he said, smiling. 'Are they still in force? Should I make a quick exit stage left?'

She shrugged noncommittally.

'You can if you want to. I'm sure Arabella would be happy to find some new people to introduce you to. I've seen so many faces I'm worn out with smiling. Not that I mind of course,' she added quickly. 'Free advertising like this doesn't come along very often.'

He glanced around him.

'I can't imagine you need to talk yourself up. The garden pretty much speaks for itself. You really did this?'

She looked up to see him gesturing around them at the

manicured lawns and brightly coloured beds.

'No need to sound so surprised,' she said. 'I told you I was a gardener.'

'I didn't realise it was on this kind of scale.'

He probably thought she grew her own herbs and had a couple of window boxes. It wouldn't be the first time. The term 'gardener' didn't really communicate the years she'd spent developing her knowledge or the management skills needed to take a project like this from start to finish.

He was watching her intently. Even his gaze seemed to touch her physically. She was so on edge she could hardly stand still and now he took a step nearer, closing the gap between them. Her stomach responded with a delicious flutter and she distracted herself with a sip of her drink.

'Why did you leave like that?' he asked softly. 'In the early hours without saying goodbye.'

It had almost been like a dream, waking up to find her gone, his mind and body aching with the night they'd spent together, her absence making it feel as if he'd imagined the whole thing.

'Dent your ego, did it?' she said. 'Used to women fawning after you misty-eyed while you backtrack and look for a way out?'

He couldn't stop a smile at that.

'Well actually, yes,' he said. 'It made an interesting change.'

She smiled back and he felt that connection he'd had with her snap back into place as if it hadn't gone. The interim six weeks dissipated. Six weeks that had been peppered with thoughts and recollections and wonderings about her that had driven him crazy. Who she was, where she lived, why she had been able to simply walk away with no comeback at all. No tracking him down, no bright carefully-casual phone messages at his work, no wondering if he might like to get together again. He'd heard it all before. Every girl except for this one, and it bothered him like an itch he couldn't reach. He couldn't help himself asking,

'You regret it?'

She tilted her chin and surveyed him with her lovely grey-green eyes, a light blush touching her cheekbones.

'None of it,' she said. 'I loved it. I But it was never going to be anything more than the one night, we both knew where we stood. I thought it was best to jump ship while I was ahead.' The way she held his gaze made heat begin to pool in his stomach. 'Also I did you a big favour. You didn't have to see me in the morning, NOT a pretty sight.'

He laughed. He'd forgotten how much he liked the freshness of the way she looked. The honey coloured hair tumbled around her face in waves and she looked softly feminine in the silk dress and heels. No mask of makeup, just freckles on her nose and lightly tanned cheekbones.

'I don't believe that for a second.'

She shrugged and glanced around her as if she was thinking of moving away, finding the next person to talk to about her work. He felt an unexpected urge to keep her engaged, unheard of for him. This reversal in circumstances didn't sit well with him. He was the one always moving on, trying to disengage. No girl he'd been with before had shown this maddening indifference.

'You didn't consider for a moment the idea of seeing me again?'

She gave him an intent look.

'Ah, but that wasn't the deal, was it? I wanted to keep it like that, perfect in my mind. I didn't want to go down to breakfast and find out things about you that I didn't like.'

'Such as?'

She looked down at her glass.

'Let's just say I'm not looking for a relationship right now,' she said. 'Not with someone like you. Not with anyone, in fact.'

He was onto the caveat instantly.

'Someone like me?'

She shook her head faintly as if to brush the comment off.

'You know virtually nothing about me.'

His voice had lifted in tone and drew a couple of interested glances. Great. A loud public discussion of her recent dalliance. What a fabulous impression that would give to prospective new contacts. She needed to dispense with this. Quickly and privately.

'Would you like to take a walk,' she said. 'Have a proper look at the garden.'

She didn't wait for a reply, simply took the gravel path down the garden, away from the buzz of the terrace. He kept pace with her.

'I didn't mean to offend you,' she said as soon as they were out of earshot. 'And I don't need an argument, not here. I'm trying to showcase my work, not show myself up.'

'Level with me then,' he said. 'What did you mean, 'someone like me'?'

Dusk was closing in now, coloured lanterns strung along the trees that lined the garden lent a softly twinkling glow to the party. Mellow jazz music was audible through the open French doors up at the house, fading softly as she led the way down the path and through the dense greenery at the end. She'd kept this area as it was, simply thinning out some of the more dominant plants and doing some cutting back to make the most of the small clearing beyond.

The warm green scent of the trees was heavy on the air, laced with smoke from the firepit being stoked back up on the flagstone area outside the house. The music was so faded now that she could hear the breeze whisper through the trees. She picked her way to the gate at the end of the garden and unlatched it. The house edged onto farmland and there was a small wood behind it that offered privacy. A five minute conversation away from her potential customers and she could get back up that garden path and carry on networking her way around the lawn. Oliver Forbes and the antsy way he made her feel was an unwelcome distraction, one she should be drawing a line under right now. If she could smooth things over with him, everything would be fine.

She walked a short distance into the wood and turned to face him. He was watching her levelly, his expression inscrutable.

'You know the reason I was at the hotel,' she said. 'I was trying to make something useful of my stupid romantic mini-break.' She sighed and leaned one hand against a tree trunk, the bark dry and rough beneath her fingers. 'My boyfriend, *ex-boyfriend,* used to work away a lot. Staying in hotels all over the country.'

She gave a wry laugh and flashed a glance at Oliver to see if he was following. His gaze didn't waver.

'Turned out he wasn't just working, if you get my drift. He was picking up women in hotel rooms.'

She saw the flash of instant understanding in his eyes.

'I get it,' he said. 'Like me. That's what you think of me, is it? The low-life cheated on you and you're pitching me at the same level.'

His expression darkened.

'You told me yourself it wasn't the first time you'd taken someone to bed that you'd only just met,' she pointed out.

He glanced skyward in a gesture of exasperation.

'The difference is, I wasn't cheating on anyone. I never have done and I never would. We were both free agents, no one was getting hurt. I didn't realise I was being judged on someone else's behaviour. I thought we were both adults and we both knew where we stood,' he added, clearly implying that *he* was the grown-up in this scenario. 'Obviously I was wrong.'

She felt suddenly very childish and an awkward pause followed as she groped for a way to regain her footing in the conversation.

'I'm sorry,' she said. 'When I woke up next to you I got this thought in my head about all those times I'd been at home, working hard, saving up for our future, while Joe was away having hotel-room-flings. I suddenly realised there might be some other girl at home waiting for you, thinking you were away working. I didn't feel right with that, so a quick exit seemed the best thing.'

'I'd told you I was single. You didn't believe me? You didn't consider waking me up to double check?'

She gave a small smile.

'I'd only just met you. You could have told me whatever you

liked. And as we'd agreed it was just the one night there wouldn't be much point double checking, would there?'

He smiled at that and tension slipped a notch. He dug his hands into his pockets and walked a half circle around her, still keeping his distance, as if thinking things over.

'And now you know there isn't any girl pining at home? Would you have behaved differently?'

He waited for her answer, looking down at the ground.

'I might not have rushed off in the early hours,' she said. 'But it was still only ever going to be the one time.'

A pause, she could hear the whisper of the leaves in the light breeze, birds singing. Her favourite sounds.

'What if I were to suggest making it more than that?' he said.

She caught her breath as the steamy details of their last encounter danced through her mind, yet the wounds from Joe's betrayal were raw enough still to make it easy to decline. The thought of dating again filled her with trepidation. She just couldn't face putting herself through it, investing all that emotion and trust only to have it crushed.

'I meant it when I said I don't want a relationship,' she said. 'I'm not in the place for that right now, not after Joe. I just want to concentrate on my work and build up the business.'

'I don't want a relationship either,' he said, voice matter-of-fact. 'Not now and not for the foreseeable. That wasn't what I was suggesting. That's why this could be perfect.'

She looked up and in his eyes she could see exactly what he meant.

'Think about it,' he said. 'Same rules as last time. No strings. No comeback. We see each other when we both want to, and when it's over we walk away. Simple.'

Her heartbeat began to climb and she leaned back against the tree because her knees seemed to have developed a strange elastic quality. Heat simmered its way from her stomach to the tops of her thighs.

This was playing with fire. The smart thing to do would be to go back up the path, carry on circulating, bag herself a few new contracts, maybe. Her mind, unconvinced, treated her to a simmering replay of their last encounter, the delectable things he'd done to her, the way he'd touched her. He had pushed her to a place so delicious she'd believed that one visit would be enough to last her forever. Now with more on offer, she found a greedy part of her surfacing that wanted to go back for more, take as much as she could get. That part of her wondered why the hell she was hesitating. Why shouldn't she enjoy life for a change instead of being at the receiving end of all the crap? There was no danger of getting in too deep here, she was in total control, after Joe the last thing she was about to do was *fall* for someone. The idea of that was laughable. This thing between Oliver and herself was *physical*, no more.

Her stomach softened like warm chocolate just at the memory of how it had been with him in his hotel room, the feel of his hands on her skin, his lips gliding over her body, his fingers exploring her. Now she knew he was single and there was no poor wronged girlfriend lurking in the background, what was to stop her? Neither of them wanted some emotionally-draining long term relationship. What the hell was so wrong in just shutting out the emotion? If men could have a no-strings, no-risk fling, and simply walk away when they'd had enough, then women could too.

'Maybe we could revise the ground rules,' she said.

Sensing victory, he moved towards her and tugged her by the hand to face him, sliding his hand around her waist. The silk dress she was wearing flowed lightly through his fingers as he explored the contours of her skin through the thin fabric. Her light flowery scent was fresh and new, like she was part of the garden, and his senses were assaulted by his sudden need for her.

In a few firm strides he backed her towards the tree trunk, green leaves hanging in fronds around them, privacy provided by the dusk and the wood, although beyond the fence the party carried on without them.

'New ground rules, then?' he said against her cheek.

Izzy automatically reached hands out to circle his neck, instantly recalling his broadness, the way it had felt to touch him, as if it had been yesterday and not weeks ago.

'Well…' she whispered into his hair '…this will not be a relationship. No going out on dates, no meeting my friends or – heaven forbid – my parents. No grief. My work comes first.'

His lips grazed her neck and she realised she was gabbling and forced herself to focus.

'And when it's over, we draw a line under it and go our separate ways. This isn't going to be friends with benefits. I have friends. It's just going to be…well… *benefits*.'

She felt him smile against her neck.

'Agreed,' he whispered, his breath warm on her skin. As he slipped a hand beneath the silk of her skirt, across the sensitive skin of her thighs, Izzy felt rough bark press against her lower back. His lips moved to meld against hers, his other hand tangling in her hair as he explored her mouth softly with his tongue. His fingers crept higher, caressing their way to the tops of her thighs and she drew in a quivering breath as his fingertips teased their way beneath her panties. Her eyes were squeezed tightly shut but she felt his mouth smile against hers in response to her reaction.

'Not here,' she squeaked. 'I'm supposed to be working.'

Yet even as she spoke the party seemed to fade to the edge of her consciousness.

Her traitorous body squirmed against him, wanting more. Her hands betrayed her, sliding lower, and she felt him catch his breath as she traced her fingers over his erection. He let out a guttural moan that filled her with excitement as she caressed him. As she began to tug at his belt, all thought of networking floating away like smoke from the firepit, he used his free hand to catch both her wrists, stopping her distraction so he could focus on her properly.

His fingers teased beneath her skirt, pulling her panties free and stroking gently at her swollen entrance until she was writhing and desperate for him to slide them inside her. He made her wait, holding her wrists lightly together at the base of her spine, revelling in indulging her completely. When he had her twisting against him, breathing hard, his hand slick with her desire, he eased his finger deep into the silken warmth of her, adding a second finger in response to her gasp, then a third, moving slowly and steadily now, his thumb circling her most sensitive spot, rhythmically moving until he felt her climax approaching in the tension of her body and the deep moan that escaped her throat. He replaced his mouth against hers, letting the sweet hiss of her breath mingle with his as he tipped her over the edge.

He was back in control. The feeling of power deep inside him as he brought her to orgasm made him want to take this further, have her again right here and now. He made himself hold back. He would make her wait now, play this out the way *he* wanted to. And when he walked away this time it would be on his terms and he would have no need to look back. He would exhaust this misplaced physical desire for her and then his mind would stop dwelling on her and he could move on.

'What about you?' she asked, trying to catch her breath. 'That didn't seem fair.' He was straightening his clothes, the expression on his face like the cat that had got the cream, finished it, and gone back in for seconds.

'Plenty of time for that,' he said.

She straightened her dress and ran a hand through her hair, wondering if what she'd just done might show on her face.

'I need to get back to the party,' she said, moving back towards the garden, opening the gate. 'You're such a bad influence, I'm meant to be networking.'

He followed her, hands in his pockets, relaxed smile on his face.

'So network,' he called after her. 'Come and work for me.'

The terrace came back into view as they walked through the greenery at the bottom of the garden. Hurricane lamps flickered on tables and people mingled in the soft light of the fire pit. The smell of woodsmoke clung to the air.

She turned back to look at him, a light frown touching her eyebrows.

'Seriously? You mean you actually want me to redesign your garden.'

'Among other things,' he said, catching her up in a couple of easy strides.

He leaned in and spoke softly in her ear.

'On these terms there doesn't need to be an end to it. No ties, no strings. Just fun. Don't you think you deserve some of that?'

'Everything has to end at some point,' she countered.

He inclined his head.

'Of course it does. So we enjoy it while it lasts, and when one or both of us are done with it we walk away. No comeback, no painful break-up, no strings. Or maybe you think you won't be able to distance yourself like that now?'

The arrogance of him! She was mesmerised by the sex, definitely. But that hunger didn't extend to wanting to get to know him or share time with him, why would it?

The flash of danger was somehow intoxicating, she felt like she was playing a role, one much more exciting than her own sensible life. But with Joe's behaviour ever on the fringe of her consciousness, she knew that a role was all it really was. *Feelings* didn't come into it.

'I need to rejoin the party now,' she said, then raised her voice as Arabella approached them. 'But I'll arrange a time for us to talk about the specifications of your garden design. Shall we take things from there?'

She held his gaze and she could see from the slight nod and the flash of a smile that he understood completely.

She wasn't saying no.

CHAPTER 5

'He's offered you a job? So what was an unemotional mutual benefit one night stand is now going to amount to you mixing business with pleasure. Since when was that ever a good idea?'

Izzy took a sip of her latte, leaned in towards Shauna across the coffee shop table and lowered her voice.

'I don't see it that way. It's a one-off job, four or five weeks at the most. I'm charging him full-whack, not mates-rates. And there's no tacit agreement that we sleep together. There was just this undertone in the conversation that made it clear: if it happens, it happens. What might go on between the two of us has nothing to do with work.'

'You're deluded,' Shauna said. 'The job is his way of keeping you exactly where he wants you.'

'For the hundredth time, this is about what *I* want, not what *he* wants. I get an easy gig one-off job that's well-paid and a no-strings fling until I get bored with it. What's not to like?'

'Watch my lips,' Shauna pointed to her own peach-glossed pout and spoke slowly and clearly. 'He no longer qualifies for the no-strings-successful-fling rule.' She held up her hands and shook her head as if she was disengaging from the whole thing. 'It will all end in tears. Almost certainly yours.'

Izzy tried and failed to stop the automatic here-we-go roll of her eyes.

'What an absolute load of crap!' she said. 'The no-strings-brilliant-fling or whatever-you-bloody-call-it rule is just some womens' magazine nonsense. I am in total control of my own life, my own decisions and my own emotions. If I want to extend the fun a bit, where the hell is the harm? Now that I know he's single and neither of us wants anything serious, who the hell is going to get hurt in a scenario like that?'

'But he's offered you a job, right?'

'Yes, but I don't see what that has to do with anything.'

Shauna threw exasperated hands up.

'You've changed the whole dynamic. You can't just mess about with the rules to fit whatever suits you. This is different. At the beginning it really was a true no-strings fling – one night, no surnames, no contact details. You *know* him now. There's an obligation involved – you have an obligation to him. Which means he is in control. When you pare it right down, what you're doing now is banging your boss.'

Izzy stared at her, speechless for a moment. Then her temper loosened her tongue and her opinion took over.

'He is NOT my boss! I am self-employed and in any case the work agreement between us is beside the point.'

'It's his way of keeping tabs on you without giving up anything in return, can't you see that? Any normal, decent bloke would have asked you out to dinner.'

'You're overlooking the fact that a dinner date with a load of poncy small talk is my idea of hell right now. I have absolutely no desire to get involved with anyone again anytime soon, not after Joe. What I want is to concentrate on building up the business and having fun. You're seeing this whole thing as being driven by Oliver and you're wrong. I'm in charge here. And with him I can I enjoy some fantastic sex without having the emotional dump. What's not to like?'

'I'm just trying to look out for you,' Shauna said quietly.

Izzy curbed her temper and lowered her voice.

'I know you are,' she said. 'And you needn't worry. The only way this is going to move forward is on my terms. I'm in total control. No emotional investment involved.'

She sounded utterly convincing. To Shauna and to herself.

***

Oliver watched as Izzy walked the perimeter of his garden, such as it was, notebook in hand, stopping occasionally to write something down. She looked very different to the smartly dressed young woman from the garden party, but there was something undeniably sexy about the scruffy jeans and work boots she was wearing with her hair tied loosely at the back of her neck, hiding the long legs and the smooth curves underneath. She looked as if she wouldn't give a toss about getting dirty, about her appearance.

The way she responded to him was beyond anything he'd known before, that lack of inhibition, her determination to experience every moment to its full. He wasn't ready to drop that yet, and when he did it would be him that dropped it, not her. Offering her this job was the perfect way of keeping her within easy reach while not having to risk any part of himself. On a sliding scale of ties it was way down below dating or friendship. A work contract had a professional detached quality that was comforting.

Plus, the garden really did need sorting out. And her work was inspired.

She was here now on his terms and based on their last meeting she would be expecting him to make some kind of move. Which was exactly why he would keep her hanging. Not that he wasn't sorely tempted, good thing in fact that he'd deliberately arranged to see her in a very tight window with work commitments on either side. However much he might want to start the add-on part of their contract, there was no way he could do that today. Let her wonder what his game was.

His staring obviously didn't escape her.

'A bit of confidence wouldn't go amiss,' she said. 'You've hardly said anything so far, you don't exactly seem excited by my ideas. You haven't handed your garden renovation over to Laurel and Hardy, you know. I do know exactly what I'm doing.'

He shook his head as if to clear it.

'Sorry. I'm perfectly satisfied that you're more than capable of handling the work. I just have a lot on my mind.'

What it might feel like to peel those work clothes off her.

'Work?'

'Always,' he said, glancing at his watch. 'I have a pressing appointment, so let's wrap this up. You can email my secretary the final details of your specification and quote. Potential start date?

'Two weeks' time,' she said. 'I have to wrap up my current job and I've got scheduled maintenance contracts to keep up for my ongoing clients.'

'Fine,' he said. 'In that case I'll be away when the work starts.

He pressed a button on his smartphone and held it in front of them. An overstuffed work schedule appeared.

Reading upside down as he clicked through the days, Izzy could see practically every day was taken up with meetings or conferences.

'Back on the seventeenth after a series of meetings in Manchester,' he said. 'So I'll be away when you get started for a day or two. When I'm around I work quite demanding hours, so I'll have my secretary supply you with a set of keys for the house, then you can come and go as you need. I assume you don't have a problem working unsupervised?'

She shook her head faintly. All about work. Whatever she'd expected, it wasn't this. No reference to anything else going on between them. Not that it was a problem, she could do professional perfectly well.

'Good. If you need to ask me something you can call my secretary.'

She noticed he didn't offer her his private mobile number or suggest she drop him a quick text.

'She'll pass a message on and I'll get back to you in due course but unless it's something major I'd prefer not to be disturbed. Just use your own judgement, you obviously know a damn sight more about gardens than I do.'

'Define something major,' she said immediately, she'd been caught out before with picky clients.

He sighed.

'Big remodelling changes that we haven't discussed today, I guess. I wouldn't be ecstatic if I came home to find you'd turned my driveway into a lawn, for example. Try not to piss off the neighbours, I can do without the grief, and I like privacy so think high fences and dense foliage. Don't go chopping down any trees without the nod from me first.'

'Something on that kind of scale would always be agreed with you at the planning stage,' she said. 'You don't need to worry, I understand exactly what you want.'

'Do you?' he said, holding her gaze with a look in his eyes that spoke of a whole different agenda.

Her heart upped the beat and she licked her suddenly-dry lips.

'Yes,' she said, returning his gaze as steadily as she could. Not easy with the distraction of major stomach flutters. The anticipation that he might reach for her at any moment seemed to have focused all her senses on his every move. Both their encounters so far had been so exciting that she couldn't help wondering how it might be next time. The thought scrambled her mind when she tried to concentrate on making notes.

He turned off the diary listing.

'You need to be careful you don't burn out,' she said.

He glanced at her and she nodded at his phone as he pocketed it.

'That diary is stuffed beyond all reason. Doesn't look like you ever take a day off.'

He smiled a little.

'I don't. Even if I'm home at the weekend there's always case files to review, stuff to be done. It's the way I like to work.'

He began to walk back to the house. She shut her notebook and followed him, picking her way over loose rubble and making a mental note to order in a skip and topsoil. There was a lot of surface rubbish to clear.

'Why put so much pressure on yourself?' she said. 'I mean, you've just spent a fortune renovating this house and now you're having the garden done. From the outside it looks like you've already made it.'

He stopped walking.

'I'll never make it, Izzy,' he said. 'I could work 24-7 for the rest of my life and I don't think I'd ever feel like that.'

For some reason the way he used her first name made her stomach give a tiny skip. His answer puzzled her.

'I don't understand. It's not like you've got to graft all the hours God sends to make ends meet. A top City lawyer? You probably make more in a month than I do in a year.'

He laughed.

'And I don't even have to wield a spade.'

She smiled back.

'I'm serious. What have you got to prove that won't let you take the occasional weekend off?'

He looked thoughtful for a moment, as if drafting a suitable answer in his head.

'It all comes down to drive, I guess,' he said. 'You can never really be certain of success,' he said. 'You're as good as your last case and things can turn around in a heartbeat. When you take your eye off the ball, that's when things slide.'

'There's nothing wrong with having a good work ethic,' she said. 'I mean the hours I've put in trying to build up some kind of paying business. It's just important to have a life outside of work too.'

'As long as it doesn't detract from work, I agree.'

She shook her head.

'All work and no play,' she said.

'I play,' he said. 'When it works for me. When play is all it is.'

The way he was looking at her, the undertone in the hazel eyes, made her heart beat up the pace as if she'd just run a few circuits of the garden. She braced herself for him to make a move, drew in a breath, and then just as quickly he snapped his gaze away and turned towards the side gate and the front of the house.

'I have to get back to work,' he said. 'Send over your spec and the contract details and I'll see you in a couple of weeks.'

She stared after him, mind whirling. He hadn't even touched her, not even to shake her hand. Her nerves were tingling, her body over-sensitised as anticipation dissolved away and worst of all, disappointment stabbed her sharply in the ribs. Definitely not allowed, disappointment would mean she actually cared what happened between them. She shoved the thought away.

Maybe a garden renovation was all he wanted after all.

CHAPTER 6

Two weeks and the only communication from her had been work related. A detailed graphic spec of his garden that impressed him in its detail and professional presentation, a contract which he'd duly signed and had returned to her along with the generous up front payment she requested. No contact with him on any social level and her continued indifference (be it real or faked) intrigued him as much as ever. The trip back from Manchester was punctuated by vague pangs of excitement, alien to him, as he thought of seeing her again tomorrow and taking control of the other aspect of their agreement.

As he pulled into the drive in front of his house in the twilight, his first reaction was irritation as he nearly ran the Maserati into a half-full skip of garden rubbish. His second reaction was a leap of anticipation deep in his stomach as he saw her van parked to the side of it.

She was still here.

He walked through the house and saw movement outside in the garden.

'Don't come any closer!' she called as he opened the kitchen door. 'The mud's horrendous.'

He picked his way into the garden. She was standing in the middle of the area that from memory was earmarked for flagstones.

Her work clothes were muddy, she wore heavy gloves and there was sand in her hair. She'd been here for two days and on the whole the garden looked worse.

'Looking good,' he said doubtfully. There were piles of rubbish and stones to the side of the space, huge bags of sand and topsoil that she'd had delivered, tools.

She pulled a face.

'It will be. It's at the transitional stage. First you strip everything back and rip everything out that needs to go and it looks at its worst. But you have to do that so it can start looking better.' She wiped the back of her hand across her face, smudging it with dirt. 'I was just finishing up. Wanted to get this cleared done so the next stage can start tomorrow. I'll be out of your way in just a minute.'

Her honey coloured hair was caught up in a loose topknot with strands escaping around her face. He realised from the diminishing quality of the light just how late it was. He was tired from his business trip and company was usually low on his list of requirements in the evening. Yet he found something else about her that drew him in, besides that physical attraction that simmered inside him. Getting dark and she was still heaving rubble about? She had a seriously demonic work ethic. And if he could relate to anything, it was that.

'Stay,' he said on impulse. 'Stay and have dinner.'

She shook her head.

'Thanks but I've got a ready-meal at home and a microwave.'

'It's no trouble. I insist.' He turned his back against any further protestations she might have and led the way into the house, talking over his shoulder. 'To be honest, I'd like the company. It's been a heavy day.'

Izzy stared at his back, unsure now of where this was going. There had been no mention of their garden party agreement since she'd started work here, no contact for two weeks beyond the signed and returned contract, and now he simply turned up and invited her to stay for dinner. No, *insisted* she stay for dinner. Was this how it was to be? Did he really want to share dinner with her, or was that just code, a hoop to jump through before he could progress this to a more physical conclusion?

She pushed away the deliberations. Physical desire for him had bubbled inside her since the garden party, as if she could discard him from her mind when she knew one night was an end to it, but now knowing there could be more the hunger for it had grown inside her. She couldn't seem to help it. And the intoxicating thought of where this might lead between them tonight made her catch her breath. Why should she care whether he wanted her company or just her touch?

She paused at the door as she looked into his pristine kitchen. He hadn't thought this through.

'Look at the state of me, Oliver. I'll walk soil and brick dust all through your house. What am I going to do, sit on a newspaper? It's been a long day and I need a shower.'

He smiled at her, that protest-melting lopsided smile.

'I've got one of those,' he said. 'You can shower while I cook. Top of the stairs, first on the left. There's a spare robe on the back of the door, you can borrow that if you've got no change of clothes.'

She hesitated a moment longer.

'Come on, by the time you get home it will be seriously late. And you have a ready-meal and a microwave?' He shook his head pityingly. 'It's dinner, not a proposal of marriage.'

She left her work boots by the back door and went upstairs.

First door on the left was the most beautifully finished bathroom she'd ever seen. Showroom polished, it looked as if she was the first person ever to use it and perhaps she was, he'd only just finished the renovations. In keeping with the Victorian fixtures, there was a beautiful roll-top bath, painted wood panelling and intricate black and white floor tiles. There were expensive bath products on the side shelf, fluffy white towels, soap in an ornate dish. But it was brochure-perfect, not remotely lived-in. There was no evidence of any female overnight guests. She stepped into the shower and let the water cascade in hot rivulets over her body, soaping her hair and washing off her day.

She toyed with putting her clothes back on – they might be dusty but to put on the bathrobe would be an unspoken message, wouldn't it? The spare bathrobe was dark blue, man sized and soft against her skin as she shrugged into it. It covered her from neck to ankle but it could be undone with one tug of the tie belt.

Her heart was beating fast. She knew perfectly well what she wanted from this situation. To wear the robe would be to make that clear to Oliver. She was in no danger here, there were no ties, no commitment, she knew his intentions and she knew her own. Her heart was safe. She padded back down the stairs barefoot.

The delicious smell of ginger, lime and coriander met her as she re-entered the kitchen. Oliver was sauteing king prawns in a heavy pan. A bowl of fragrant rice stood on the glass table at one side of the kitchen, next to it a salad. A bottle of ice-cold white wine, condensation clinging to it, stood alongside and as she crossed the room he poured her a glass, then one for himself.

Oliver's fingers touched hers as he handed her the glass and he fought to keep his composure at the sight of her. Swamped in the huge bathrobe she looked fragile, her skin pink from the shower, her hair damp, already reverting to its usual waves, caught up on her head with damp tendrils escaping and clinging to the skin of her neck. Not a scrap of make-up on her face, he could see every tiny freckle. Desire began to pool hotly in his abdomen. Had he ever come across someone who appealed to him so deeply on a physical level? The knowledge that he could extend one finger and pull that robe apart, the thought that beneath it she was naked, made him want to discard the food and have her right now.

She sat down at the table. Obviously for her, dinner was more of a pull. He served the meal and sat down opposite her.

She speared a prawn, forked up some rice, tasted it. He watched her savouring it, his own appetite dissipating despite his long day.

'This is delicious,' she said.

'No need to sound so surprised.'

She grinned.

'Sorry. I'm always impressed by people who can cook, especially when it looks like you've just thrown it together, because I'm so rubbish at it myself. I can grow the stuff but when it comes to cooking it…' she pulled a face. 'Where did you learn to cook like this?'

An unexpected flash of childhood. In the kitchen, one eye on his younger brother, the other on the stove. His mother working her second job.

'Circumstances really,' he said. 'I picked up the basics from my mother when I was a kid and after that I learned by having a go.'

A smile of approval.

'Your mum was forward-thinking then, equipping you for the world,' she said. She pulled a face. 'Traditional roles were very much the thing in my house.'

'He hunts it, she cooks it?'

'Exactly. My mother was – is – Fifties cupcake housewife living in the wrong decade. She had a sheltered strict upbringing and it indoctrinated her for life. Dad brought home the money and that's exactly the line where his responsibility ended. My mother did everything else. Literally. All the cleaning, all the cooking, dealing with me.'

'She didn't go out to work? I thought maybe one or both of your parents might have been into gardening too, since you're so obsessed with it.'

'I am NOT obsessed with it! And no, my parents aren't gardeners. They're bemused by what I do. We didn't even have a garden when I was growing up – we had a little terrace house with a concrete back yard where my mum used to hang washing. It backed onto a cobbled alleyway where the bins were kept. Not so much as a blade of grass in sight.'

'How on earth did you fall into garden design then, if you

weren't encouraged by someone? It's a bit…vocational, isn't it?'

She was smiling a little down at her plate, pushing food around with her fork.

'My mum sees me in my work stuff and my steel toe-caps she thinks I'm some kind of labourer.' She raised an eyebrow. 'Or maybe a lesbian. As if I've lost all sense of femininity. But then what do you expect from someone who powdered her nose every day ready for when my father got home. Not that he appreciated it.'

He didn't miss the sudden harshness of her voice. He felt a flash of empathy with her over her parents.

'She's never really taken the time to understand what I really do. Yes, there's a lot of physical work but at the base level it's really a creative job. Turning something that's old, or a mess, or that doesn't work into something lovely and pleasing.'

'So how did you get into it then? Is there a career path?'

She smiled at him.

'Come on,' he encouraged. 'I had to tick all the right boxes to get where I am. University degree, Legal Practice Course, period of on-the-job training. What happens with gardening, do you suddenly wake up and discover you have a green thumb?'

She laughed.

'It wasn't like a sudden epiphany, I just always enjoyed being out of the house. We had a park a few streets away and I loved the feeling of space there, my house was so claustrophobic you can't imagine. Then when I hit my teens I looked for a Saturday job, just like everyone else.'

As she smiled up at him his heart flipped softly at the delight in her eyes.

'I started working at a garden centre,' she said.

He grinned, unable to help himself.

'From your beatific expression I thought you'd got a Saturday job at a sweet shop at the very least.'

'Very funny. This was better than sweets. I loved it. I loved being outside, I loved handling the plants, developing displays, advising customers. I just knew this was something I could love and that I'd never get tired of – you know?'

He didn't know. Work for him was about validation and security. About money. The law hadn't chosen him, he had chosen it. There was no vocation involved.

'When I left school I went full-time at the garden centre and took a few courses at college and then I started doing one-off jobs for people in my spare time. Maybe they wanted their beds sorted out, or a pond putting in. I just picked up small jobs and taught myself as I went along. It wasn't easy, I made lots of mistakes but slowly the business grew and I began to bring people in to do things I couldn't, laying patios, that kind of thing. It's slowly developed into more of a project management thing, with me doing what I can and subcontracting the rest. But I'm in control of all of it. It's the best thing. I never get tired of it.'

Her attitude to work was something he couldn't help admiring and responding to. He had the same drive himself but without the job satisfaction. He'd deliberately chosen a profession, something he knew would pay well if he worked at it. People always need lawyers. His lack of enthusiasm must have shown in his face.

'You're looking at me like you think I'm mad,' she said.

'I was just thinking that I envy you,' he said. 'I've never really been in my work for the love of it.'

'I can't imagine many lawyers are,' she said. 'Unless you're one of those altruistic human rights types, fighting for the underdog.'

'I wouldn't be living somewhere like this if I was,' he said. 'There's no money in altruism.'

She was forking up rice and salad, not looking at him, and the sudden urge to elaborate came from nowhere.

'My work ethic probably has a lot to do with my father,' he said.

She finished her mouthful without looking up, and he thought with momentary relief that she would make no comment. He shouldn't be talking about personal stuff, not with her. Then she spoke,

'Is he a lawyer too, then?'

He couldn't stop his cynical laugh and she looked up in surprise.

'Did I say something funny?'

He shook his head.

'I'm sorry. I'm not laughing at you. It's just the idea of my father working for a living.'

Izzy could hear the bitterness in his voice and her curiosity instantly sharpened.

'You aren't close then?'

'Weren't close,' he corrected. 'He died eight years ago.'

'I'm sorry,' she said, knowing it was the stock response and wishing she knew some other way to react. But how else could you react when you barely knew someone? You couldn't commiserate, not without it sounding hollow and insincere.

He waved a hand dismissively.

'Don't be. To be honest his death didn't have much of an impact.' He paused. 'He didn't make much of an impact when he was alive so I suppose it follows that he wouldn't exactly knock me flying with his death.'

'Were he and your mum still together?' she asked before she could check herself, and sudden heat flared in her cheeks and neck. What was she doing? She held up a hand immediately to stop him. 'I'm really sorry, I'm so nosy. I didn't mean to pry.'

He dismissed her with a shake of his head.

'By the time he died they'd been apart for a few years, but she stuck it out for a long time while me and my kid brother were growing up.' He glanced up at her. 'Bit like your mum by the sound of it – I think she thought throwing the towel in would mean she was a failure.'

Her mother flashed into her mind. Keeper of appearances. Avoider of gossip. Her heart softened towards Oliver a little in spite of her guard.

'What was your father like then?' she asked tentatively. 'Since he wasn't a lawyer.'

'He was a waste of space. He never held a job down for longer than five minutes. He had no drive, no ambition. My mother worked two jobs to keep a roof over our heads, sometimes three, and he never seemed to feel an ounce of guilt about that. He had no qualms about taking the household money to the pub. Then he'd sit there with his cronies moaning about his misfortune. He thought the world owed him a living.'

'I'm sorry,' she said again. Stock response again, as if it would help or matter. How unnatural it felt to have been with this man on such a deep physical level and yet to be picking her way over the eggshells of conversation for fear of offending him.

Oliver pushed his plate to one side and the subject of his father along with it. If they had to talk, make it about her.

'So all this effort you've poured in – what's it all aimed at?' he said, topping up her glass of wine.

'Building up my business of course. I've worked hard on my client list, managed to whittle down a list of subcontractors I can rely on. Weeded out the cowboys.'

'I mean longer-term. What do you aim at?'

She looked down at her meal, put her cutlery together on the plate and pushed it aside.

'Same thing as everyone I supposed. Family and kids one day. My own house in a place where there isn't too much concrete about.' She leaned towards him with a small smile and he caught the soft vanilla scent of soap from the shower. 'A big garden,' she said.

'And is that what you were planning for with your ex?'

Sudden tension in her shoulders and the tilt of her jaw as she held his gaze. Then she relaxed slightly. He could almost see the click as she decided to confide in him and it touched him somehow. Touched him deep in his chest where mutual trust was an unknown, untested entity. Trust meant mutual reliance and Oliver Forbes let no one depend on him. It was the only way to be sure of never letting anyone down.

'*I* was,' she said. 'Turned out it wasn't quite so important to him.'

She toyed with her wine glass.

'We were saving up for a deposit for a house,' she said. 'I rent a tiny little studio flat at the moment.' She gave him a wry smile. 'No garden.'

He nodded acknowledgement.

'But it doesn't matter much because I get to spend all day in lovely gardens like yours, or at least like yours will be. I was looking forward to having one of my own though, I've got a massive folder full of ideas and design plans. We agreed we'd both work really hard for a couple of years, save like crazy and then get on the housing ladder.'

So it had been pretty serious then. He saw now why a short-term fling might have its appeal after the demise of something like that.

'And it didn't work out,' he prompted.

She sighed and shook her head.

'A couple of months ago I picked up his mobile phone when it rang – he was out of the room.' She uttered a laugh that was a bit too small to really pull off. 'I don't know who was more shocked, me or the girl on the other end. She had no idea I even existed. Turned out his nights away weren't all work and no play, if you get my drift. And she wasn't a one-off. When I finally got him to come clean he admitted one-night-stands were par for the course.'

'I'm sorry,' he said, wanting to say that the guy was a moron, but painted into a hypocritical corner by the fact he'd taken her to bed without knowing her last name and with no follow-up plans.

He stood up and took their plates to the counter.

'It really was about revenge after all then, that night at the hotel with me,' he said, with his back to her.

'Revenge would imply that I gave a damn about him,' she said. 'That I felt I had a point to prove.'

'And you didn't. You don't?'

'No.' As he turned she looked up and gave a small smile. 'Maybe a little bit at the hotel. I can't say it wasn't nice to feel reckless for once. And when someone cheats on you, there's this automatic conclusion that it's because of something that's lacking in *you*. Doesn't matter how hard you try and keep the moral high ground, all the time there's this feeling that if you'd been everything he wanted he never would have strayed.' She toyed with her wine glass. 'That night was about that more than anything. About feeling like I was desirable instead of disappointing.'

The self-doubt in her voice tugged at his heart and before he could check himself he had discarded the plates. He was back across the kitchen in a couple of swift paces, acting on impulse, kneeling down in front of her so his eyes were level with hers.

'How can you imagine yourself anything but desirable?'

She only looked at him, and he lifted a hand to stroke her hair back from her cheek as he leaned in to kiss her.

His lips against hers, he pulled her gently to her feet. Sparks tingled through Izzy right down to her toes as she felt him tug at the tie-belt of the robe, then his hands were beneath it, stroking tantalisingly across her bare skin. She let her fingers sink into the thickness of his hair, moved the other hand to open the buttons of his shirt then pull at his belt.

As her robe fell to the floor he kicked her chair to one side and leaned around her. She heard the tinkle of china and clatter of cutlery as he swept the table settings randomly aside, then his hands were sliding back around her, firm beneath her thighs as he lifted her, easing her up to sit on the edge of the table. Her legs were splayed either side of him, the glass of the table smoothly cold against the back of her thighs.

He slid his lips downwards to the hollow of her neck, tantalisingly lower through the hollow between her breasts. Eyes squeezed tightly shut, every sense tuned into him in anticipation of his next move, she waited, breath held as he took a sideways detour with his mouth, tracing kisses over her breast until he closed his lips softly over her nipple. She tensed for a moment then breathed out in a soft moan as he sucked gently and slid his tongue back and forth across its hard tip, sending hot sparks down her body to simmer between her thighs.

She clutched agonisingly, deliciously at his hair as he continued his slow, deliberate course downwards, tracing her skin with lips and fingers. Eyes closed, her head tipped back to the ceiling, she soaked up every drop of sensation. She vaguely sensed him stretching to reach behind her for something on the table, and he parted her thighs with one hand. She yielded, so swept up in the sensations he invoked that she could do nothing else. Then her eyes widened and she let out an audible gasp as he suddenly pressed the cold back of a spoon against her exposed core. Its icy smoothness against her hot sensitive skin intensified every delicious sensation and as she writhed against it he replaced the coldness with his own mouth, the contrast of his warm breath sending her arousal spinning to impossible heights. Had she ever wanted anyone or anything so much?

He circled the nub of her slowly with his tongue, as his fingers stroked their way lower still, teasing her, building the ache for him deep inside her.

Her breath quickened as her climax approached. She could feel herself teetering deliciously on the brink of it, locked fingers in his thick hair to try and keep his tongue in that sweet spot long enough to tip her over. Yet with some sixth sense, in tune to her every response, he then retreated softly, again and again until she heard herself cry out for him.

Instantly he was on his feet. A moment to catch her breath as he freed himself and ripped open a condom and then in one quick movement he replaced his fingers with his erection, pressing forward into her in a smooth thrust right to her very core, filling her up and rushing her senses at the same time.

His lips found hers again and he kissed her greedily. She could smell the musky scent of his aftershave on hot skin as she let her hands slide down his back over rigid muscle, drinking in the scent, the taste, the feel of him, it seemed her every sense had room for nothing but him. They moved now together as one, her hands sliding down to push him as deeply into her as she could, long slow strokes which drove her spinning back and then dizzyingly, deliciously forward. As it tore through her she cried her ecstasy into his mouth and felt him tense against her as he let himself tip over the edge beside her.

CHAPTER 7

It seemed that even the most impromptu unplanned physical encounters were just like everything else in life. If they took place more than a few times elements of routine began to seep in. She'd been with Oliver three times now since that hot night on the kitchen table, each time punctuated by the same events. He would return home from work early evening, would cook something and ask her to join him, and afterwards things would go further.

Like the garden, things between them were gradually becoming more defined, more detailed.Maybe routine was just inevitable. It didn't mean she was getting sucked in and losing her heart. Yes she thought about him a lot, but that was natural – right? She was working on his bloody garden. And a routine might be slipping in but it was still one that fitted around everything else. It was clear that Oliver's priorities hadn't changed. He was still working all hours, gone before she arrived in the morning and never back until the light was fading at the end of the day. Still putting work first. Maybe he was incapable of doing anything else. She certainly wasn't important enough to make him deviate from that.

Late afternoon, nearly four weeks into the project and the garden had turned a corner from looking worse to better. The air was hot and damply heavy with the threat of rain as she arrived there after having sorted out a lawn treatment for one of her regular clients. She was anxious to get back before the threatening rain kicked in, to make sure it would cause as little disruption as possible to the work still needed. As she got out of the van and slammed the driver's door the first fat drops began to fall, warm not cold, the summer sky pushed out by the scurrying dark clouds. Summer storms, her enemy. They could hold up a project for days, turn beds ready for planting into bogs, unseat flagstones that were waiting to be sealed, warp untreated wood. As she ran for the narrow wrought iron gate at the side of the house, her vest and shorts began to soak through.

At the entrance to the garden she stood and stared in exasperation. The plants she'd ordered had been delivered while she was gone, simply left laid out in pallets behind the house. Baby plants were being pelted into squashed submission by the rain, compost waterlogging while she watched. She needed to get the whole lot under cover, ten minutes ago. She'd worn flip-flops in the van and in her rush hadn't changed into her boots, so her feet soaked and slipped as she fumbled Oliver's kitchen door key out of her shorts pocket and began to load herself up with plants and deposit them on the gleaming kitchen floor, trekking back and forth again and again. Muddy water soaked across the expensive new ceramic tiles but she'd worry about that later.

At a sound behind her she turned and blinked hard to clear the rain from her eyes. Oliver. Home hours early. Good grief, had someone died? The pelting rain allowed no more than that fleeting thought.

Oliver stared at her, heedless of the torrent of rain soaking his clothes. Her hair was dripping strings, droplets of water clung to her eyelashes and her shirt was transparent, revealing a lacy push-up bra underneath. Just the sight of her like that was enough to get him started.

'Don't just bloody well stand there!' she snapped. 'Give me a hand!'

Taking in what she was doing, he helped her grab the pallets of plants and stack them in the kitchen, forcing himself to ignore the smears of mud and water that were spreading across his pristine floor. She was picking her way across the planks that crisscrossed the half-finished garden, put there to make working on it easier, grabbing tools that had been left out, when her flip-flops slipped on the wet wood. Even though he was feet away he made an automatic lunge to catch her as she pinwheeled her arms, and when he failed she sat down with an ungainly splattering thump in one of the waterlogged beds. Mud soaked her shorts and splattered across her cheek.

She stared up at him from her sitting position and burst into giggles. Picking his way over to her, feet sliding everywhere, his own clothes dripping, he held out an arm to pull to her feet, and as she drew level with him, face tipped up to look into his, smile still on her face at her own clumsiness, something visceral clutched deep inside him so strongly that it took his breath away. His own laugh faded on his lips. Rain ran down her forehead and cheeks. She was a dirt-covered mess. Had he ever wanted anyone so damn much?

Heedless of the mud that coated her back and now squirted between his fingers, he slid hands beneath her t-shirt, across wet skin, his mouth groping for hers, tasting rainwater on her lips and breathing in the scent of her warm damp skin. Hunger for her swept through him at a rampaging pace that crushed everything else from his consciousness. Tugging her t-shirt over her head, he pushed her bra up roughly and cupped her breasts in his palms, lightly pinching the nipples between his fingers, her gasp arousing him all the more. He wanted her urgently now. The rain, cool and sweet, sluiced over the soaked back of his shirt.

She had loosened his belt and unzipped his trousers, freeing his erection as she sank to her knees in the mud, and then he felt her warm breath on him as she took him into her mouth. The pleasure was so acute he failed to stop a moan, and then she was moving with deliberate tantalising slowness, her tongue sliding over his length as she sucked gently. He tangled his hands in her wet hair, the unfamiliar sensation of outdoor freedom, cool air and rain on his skin mingled with the heat curling through his body, enveloping his mind as she moved her lips in a rhythmic friction that drove him crazy.

With a monumental effort, he tugged her to her feet, wanting her now, right this second. He grabbed her hand and pulled her, stumbling through the mud and water, both of them half-dressed, into the kitchen where he had condoms. As he shrugged out of his wet clothes and readied himself, she peeled off her soaked shorts and panties, then she planted her hand firmly on his chest and pushed him, holding his gaze steadily with her own, backwards until he hit one of the chairs beside the table.

'Sit down,' she said, and as he did she climbed into his lap and lowered herself inch by delicious inch onto him. Toes on the floor, she rolled her hips and began to grind against him, her hands cool against his cheek as she held his face and kissed him, responding to his every move as if she had some sixth sense, speeding up and slowing down until she'd teased him to the point of madness. He caressed the curve of her bottom, slid hands over the softness of her back, slightly gritty under his fingers from the drying mud, let her ride him on her terms until he could take no more. Then, standing up and sliding hands beneath her, he walked the few paces to lean her back against the kitchen wall. He screwed her against it, crushing her mouth with his own, her arms around his neck, her long legs crossed behind his waist as he drove into her again and again, waiting for her cry of satisfaction before he let himself release the last tendrils of control.

***

Showered and in his bed, the rain continued to pelt against the high windows, giving the bedroom a cosy feel.

'Thanks,' she said.

He propped himself up on one elbow, looked down at her on the pillow, unruly waves of hair pooled around her face.

'What for?'

'Helping me out with the plants. Not getting annoyed at the mess in your kitchen. Plenty of clients wouldn't have been so understanding if I'd walked muddy water into their house.'

'Is that all I am, a client?' he said. He watched for her reaction, saw the grey-green eyes soften with laughter.

'Are you saying you want it to be more?'

He shrugged.

'We could be friends,' he said.

'Friends?'

'Friends with benefits,' he said, grinning. 'Ringing the changes from just benefits.'

He meant it light-heartedly but as she smiled up at him his heart turned over softly.

'Stay,' he said then, before he could stop himself. Already desire was coursing through him again. He had expected her to be a longer-term extension to his usual one-night-stands. He certainly hadn't counted on this thing with her being such a laugh. Hadn't counted on looking forward to seeing her the way he did. When had he last finished work earlier than six? Bumped work for something, anything else? He'd taken his eye off the ball with her and that was dangerous, he should be distancing himself, but then he would be soon enough. The end of the garden contract loomed ahead of them and he insisted to himself that he was simply making the most of the situation until then. This thing between them would come to a natural end then.

'For dinner?' She looked up at him from the pillow.

'For dinner, then the night. Stay over.'

A pause. Just a momentary one, yet still a pause. She hadn't automatically dismissed it.

Maybe this was worse, because now she dismissed it after consideration. And of course she was right to.

'I can't.' She looked up at him with a smile and then threw the covers back and crossed the room, stepped into old jeans, pulled a work t-shirt over her head. No bra. She'd left a spare set of clothes here, a spare pair of shoes. But no toothbrush, no cosmetics. Nothing that could be construed as anything more than work convenience.

'Can't or won't?'

She looked across at him, a smile playing about her lips.

'Both,' she said. 'I've got my own place. And it doesn't fit the ground rules.'

He sat up in bed.

'Sod the ground rules,' he said.

She was into her shoes now, an old scuffed pair of Converse. She leaned against the bedroom door jamb.

'I can't sod the ground rules, Oliver,' she said. 'I can be friends but I can't do that.' She blew a kiss across the room. 'See you tomorrow.'

She left the room before he could say anything else to persuade her, he listened to her clattering down the stairs and slamming the back door. That sensation he'd felt back at the hotel, waking up to find she'd gone, flooded back. The feeling of being short-changed, of losing control.

Izzy sat in the van for a few moments, fighting the desire to go back inside. The end was coming into sight. She mentally calculated, wondering what start date she should give to the clients for her next job. A couple more days? A week?

There would be no reason soon for contact with Oliver. She shoved away the strange feeling of emptiness that thought provoked. The whole delicious situation had given her a feeling of power that was like nectar after Joe's betrayal, of course it was that she didn't want to give up. It had nothing, absolutely nothing to do with any misplaced feelings for him. OK maybe they'd become friends, just by talking over the last few weeks they'd got to know each other, but that didn't change a thing. No strings stood.

She would put the finishing touches to the garden in the next few days and walk away without looking back.

CHAPTER 8

'All done,' she said, leading the way back up the garden. Where the piles of rubble and rubbish had been there was now a softly shaped lawn, bordered with flowers and shrubs designed to give greenery all year round. The trees had been cut back, but not enough to remove the privacy that was so important to him. Next to the house was a circular flagstone terrace with a wrought-iron table.

'I hope you're pleased with the end result,' she said, to fill the silence.

'I love it,' he said. 'I can hardly believe it's the same space as it was a few weeks ago. You're good. Definitely worthy of recommendation.'

Even in her sadness that this was coming to an end, she felt a flush of pride the way she always did when someone praised her work. Reputation was everything.

'Thanks.'

'I'll have the payment wired to you first thing tomorrow.'

'I just need to round up my tools and stack them in the van and then I'll be out of your hair.' *For good*, she nearly added, but didn't.

He shook his head, dismissive.

'Do that after dinner.'

'Are you sure that's a good idea?'

She'd tried hard to mentally distance herself since he'd come home early two days ago. Friends with benefits was harder to walk away from than benefits, but she meant to do it.

'One last night,' he said, looking at her steadily, his hazel eyes holding her gaze.

She nodded.

'Let's go out,' he said.

She stared at him, hardly believing her ears.

'Out?'

'For a drink.'

He stepped briefly into the kitchen to grab his keys, then locked the door and led the way to his car. She followed him in her jeans and converse. He'd never taken her anywhere. Since the hotel they'd only ever been together at this house. What did this mean? Did he want to take things to the next level? The thought made her stomach flutter with excitement that she couldn't acknowledge. She glanced down at herself as she climbed into the pristine Maserati. At least she wasn't in her steel toe-caps. She shook away the self-consciousness.

It was just a drink. It meant nothing.

***

'Order whatever you like,' he said, taking her right back to that first night in the hotel restaurant.

'What's this about, Oliver,' she said. 'You didn't need to do this, you know. I don't need a steak dinner to say thank you, it was a business transaction.'

'It's our last night,' he said, putting into words what they both knew.

'And you wanted to signify that in some way?' She took a sip of her drink. Had she really thought this might mean something? Why did she even want it to? She forked up some fries and swallowed them quickly to stop the stupid churning in her stomach. This was playing out exactly as it was meant to. As they'd *both* meant it to from the start.

'I thought it might be nice.' His face was inscrutable, his tone stilted.

Nice? The easy banter they'd developed was missing, presumed dead. And didn't that make sense? Easy banter and drinks in pubs didn't sit well between them because those things belonged to people in proper full relationships. Weeks on and they were basically still living that one-night-stand. Their relationship began with sex, and that was how it was going to end. Apparently there was no room for anything more than that between them.

She realised with a flash of clarity what this whole encounter had really been about for her.

'Maybe it's a good thing that this is ending,' she ventured. 'I've got my head straight now. All this time I've been thinking this thing between us has been about Joe. Maybe I felt like I was owed some fun, maybe I wanted to be the one playing the game for a change. But these last few weeks I've been thinking more and more about my parents too and that's unusual for me because we're not close.' She shrugged. 'Maybe this whole fling has had more to do with them than with Joe.'

He watched her as she toyed with her wine glass. Fidgeting. Uncomfortable. Oliver Forbes didn't do shoulders to cry on or sympathetic ears. He should be making a swift exit right now before he got sucked into anyone else's problems. What the hell had he been thinking, taking her out for a drink, moving the goalposts? He couldn't do full-on relationships, already the ease of their company was unravelling. If he let this go further, let them get closer beyond that physical connection, how long would it be before he walked away and hurt her?

'How do you mean?'

'Joe wasn't right for me,' she said. I think I even knew that before his cheating smacked me between the eyes. I wanted that relationship to work, Oliver, I wanted to be part of a couple where both of us gave everything to the partnership, where we were a team. My father had a string of affairs and my mum turned a blind eye. One of them even turned up at the house once, when I was about ten. She had blonde curly hair and she wore a lot of make-up. And do you know what my mother did?'

He shook his head, thinking how confusing that must have been for a kid.

'She invited her in and made tea.' She uttered a strangled little laugh that tugged at his heart and before he could think about it he reached out and squeezed her hand.

'When I found out about Joe I threw him out of my flat. I grabbed as much of his stuff as I could and lobbed it into the street after him. The last thing I gave a damn about was what people might think. But she didn't want the neighbours to gossip.'

'Perhaps she was staying put for you,' he said. 'Trying to give you a stable home life.'

She shook her head dismissively.

'She's still with him, years after I left home. It's never mentioned. She was, and still is, a doormat, Oliver. I swore I would never be that, but look at how I ended up. Joe did exactly the same to me, it had been going on for months. *Months.* I'd been holding it together at home, saving, planning our future. You'd think I of all people would be able to see through him, see what he was doing, but I didn't have a clue.'

She sighed.

'I've never understood my mother's behaviour, why she would put up with that. Maybe this whole thing has been about trying to work that out. Maybe there was a bit of me wanting to be the other woman for once, wanting to be on that fun side of the fence just to see if it was any better. That's what this fling has been about. You have no idea how out of character this has been for me.'

She ran a hand distractedly through her hair.

'You have nothing to prove, Izzy,' he said.

She looked down at her hand, still enclosed in his.

'You're not to blame for Joe's behaviour.' He paused, then added,

'Or your father's. It's not because of anything lacking in you.'

She pulled her hand away immediately, her cheeks burning because he'd somehow managed to see inside her mind.

'Let's go home,' he said.

***

Up in his bedroom the knowledge that this was the last time hung over them like a cloud. As he took his jacket off she could stand it no longer.

'Maybe I should just go, Oliver. Maybe we just call it quits while we're ahead. The garden's done.' She gave him a small smile. 'We're done too.'

He shook his head, walked towards her.

'It doesn't have to be like that.'

'I think maybe it does. Maybe this whole thing has been a mistake. This has been me putting myself out there trying to prove I'm good enough, sexy enough to be the other woman, to be some cheap fling. Maybe I should have stayed home, like the good little wife. Like my mother. After all, Joe always came back to me in the end.'

She made a move for the door. In two quick strides he'd grabbed her from behind and enveloped her in his arms. He ignored her angry struggles and spoke into her hair.

'That's exactly where you're wrong, Izzy. You're too good to put down, too good to leave.'

He turned her gently in his arms and lifted a hand to her cheek, stroked a tendril of hair back and watched as she covered his hand with her own and turned her face into his fingers, eyes closed, as if to soak up his every touch. His heart turned over softly. He wanted to stroke every ounce of self-doubt out of her.

In a rush of sudden comprehension Oliver saw that this was no longer about having the best time with the least investment. Yes, it had started out as exactly that, but somewhere along the way when he'd turned his back it had become much more. It was no longer about jumping through hoops to get to the physical, the job, the dinners a means to an end. He'd begun to enjoy the damn hoops just as much as the culmination of their evenings together.

Sex with her was different. The anonymity was long gone. It had become about pleasing her, sharing an experience, taking her to a level she'd never been to, wanting to better that and keep on bettering it. Benefits was long gone. Friends with benefits didn't really cover it. Somehow he'd taken his eye off the ball and found himself wanting even more. And although it scared the living daylights out of him he was powerless to stop it.

With infinite slowness he slid a hand around her waist, pulling her against him as he found her mouth with his. The stroke of her hands through his hair and over his skin thrilled him. Different this time. The usual passion still simmering there, but this time with a new depth that tugged deep in his chest. He kissed his way softly along her jawline, then back to the softness of her mouth, exploring with his tongue, wanting to taste and feel and experience every part of her. Her hands were beneath his shirt, the touch of her fingers on his skin touching his soul. There was physical pleasure and then there was this. A whole new plane, the desire to make her happy, to make her smile and laugh as well as sigh with pleasure. The thought crashed into his mind, sending him into a dizzying mental tailspin.

This was not just sex.

For the first time ever it was not just about the physical thrill of it for him. This was making love. He drew exquisite pleasure not just from the physical sensations but from pleasing her and being with her. He lifted her in his arms and carried her to the bed, laid her gently down and eased her clothes off, kissing each new patch of skin as he exposed it until she was squirming with desire. Knitting her fingers with his own beside her head, he held her grey-green gaze as he thrust smoothly inside her, watched the close of her eyes and the pleasure on her face with every slow deliberate stroke he made.

Her legs curled around him, binding him to her like silky ropes, her free hand sliding down from the base of his spine to push him deeper and deeper into her. Her hunger for him thrilled him on a level he had never known. With each stroke he pulled back almost entirely before thrusting back inside her, never wanting it to stop, hearing in the soft hiss of her breath that he was pushing her towards those delicious heights. He could see in the depths of her eyes pure pleasure with a twist of sadness, and knew it was because this would be the last time. How far they'd come from that no-strings night in the hotel.

He was in total control of this. He could perpetuate it if that was what he wanted. He simply had to find a way that minimised risk.

Afterwards, he left the room for a moment and returned, glass of water in hand to find her curled up in his bed, honey coloured hair spilling over the pillow, long eyelashes lying against her cheek, sound asleep. He wanted her as much as ever.

This didn't need to be the end. He would tell her in the morning.

CHAPTER 9

Izzy grabbed the broom from where it leaned against the side of the house and gave the circular terrace a final once-over. Not that it needed it.

She had hidden her shock at waking up in his bed by taking a superfast shower and going downstairs to the garden without giving him a moment to speak. Fifteen minutes to finish up and she would be gone from here. Gone from him.

Only now it was over did she feel the wrench. She knew she was in too deep. Her heart twisted in her chest at the thought of not seeing him again. Had she felt this level of sadness when it had ended with Joe? That somehow seemed so distant to her now. And of course the downside of falling for the other half of your no-strings fling was that you couldn't state your feelings because that would mean flouting the very rules on which you were together. She'd misread his behaviour last night, she wasn't about to do it again.

She'd gone into this with her eyes open, had set the terms out herself at the outset, and reinforced them along the way. Could she really blame him for sticking to that when their arrangement – because that's what it really was – was over?

She turned as he stepped through the French windows onto the terrace, no longer overgrown and rubbish-filled now, but an intimate leafy space. To sit here at the wrought-iron table and chairs was to feel completely private, out of reach of the rest of the world. Her cheeks reddened a little as she recalled how the cool air had felt against her bare skin out here and realised privacy was probably the whole point of his design request. No doubt he would be wining and dining his conquests out here in future. He was dressed for work. Ready to go.

She replaced the broom. It was none of her business.

'I'm done,' she said, forcing a smile and brushing her hands against her jeans. 'I'll just collect up my last few tools and bits and I'll be out of your hair.'

He leaned against the wall, watching her, the hazel eyes crinkling lightly at the corners, his smile curling the left side of his mouth in that gorgeous way that she'd stupidly come to think of as hers. Serve her right, she'd known the risks.

'Izzy, I don't want to quit seeing you,' he said.

Her heart leapt.

'Really?' she whispered, smiling up at him as he took a step closer and slipped an arm around her waist.

Excitement bubbled up inside her. He felt the same!

Then he felled her heart with one swift add-on sentence.

'I've found you another job.'

***

The joy of moments earlier slipped away, replaced by the breath-shortening crush of disappointment in her chest and a rising burn in her cheeks. Deserved embarrassment at her own stupid pride.

Last night's reassurances meant nothing after all, because still all he wanted from her was the fun part, the no strings part. If nothing had been lacking in her he would want more, wouldn't he? The fact he didn't made what had seemed so delicious and exciting at the beginning seem suddenly cheap and nasty.

Not noticing, he carried on outlining his plans.

'You know the big white house at the end of the road, the one with all the overbearing greenery out front?'

'Yes.' Her voice sounded like it belonged to someone else.

'I've got you a new contract lined up. I know the owner through work and he mentioned they wanted to overhaul their garden, so I recommended you. His wife came and checked out my garden at the weekend and they can't wait to meet you and get started on roughing out some designs. They were just blown away with what you did here.'

She couldn't speak. Her mouth felt like it was filled with sand.

His smile faltered a little at her silence.

'Are you not listening? I've got you a new contract two seconds down the road. We can have dinner together, hang out, you can stay over when you want to. What do you think?'

Had she actually believed for a moment there that he might feel the same way as her? She'd assumed that staying overnight had made the difference, that he'd seen it as some kind of tentative commitment between them. It had meant nothing, just an extension of the agreement they'd had before. The feeling of sudden isolation dragged her spiralling downwards, she'd presumed to know his mind. She of all people who knew in spades that you could never really know anyone. To think you did was to set yourself up for a kick in the teeth.

Her father. Joe. And now Oliver. Did she have some kind of blind spot?

The goalposts hadn't moved an inch for him after all. The tenderness, the closeness she thought she felt were illusions, a mistake. He thought she still wanted nothing more than no-strings sex. And she'd read more into it because he'd cooked her a few meals, encouraged her to stay the night, talked her up over Joe and her parents.

He'd basically found a way of prolonging their affair that required no further commitment whatsoever. Nice and safe and arms-length. What would happen when this contract was up and she'd built the white house couple a lovely new garden? Would she be presented with yet another neighbour with a yard full of weeds so that Oliver could keep his precious independence and yet still have the part of her he wanted – the physical part? Emotions need not apply.

She shook her head and withdrew her arms from his neck. Stepped back into her personal space.

'I can't do it,' she said.

She moved to start packing the last of the garden items away, concentrated on stacking some seed trays. She felt his eyes on her and glanced up. The crushed look in his eyes tugged at her heart but she knew it for what it was – disappointment that his supply of no-strings sex was being turned off. Nothing more. She supposed he was bemused as to why she hadn't just bitten his arm off and could she really blame him for that? This was what she'd said she wanted all along, after all. A no-strings fling. All he'd done was find a way to prolong it, with another nice gardening contract thrown in.

It was no longer enough.

'Why not?'

She carried on packing up her stuff, knowing what this meant and fighting the cold tendrils of disappointment that snaked their way through her. This was the end.

He touched her arm softly.

'I don't understand. I thought you'd be made up. What's wrong?' He took the pile of seed trays out of her hands and tugged her across to the wall, sat down and pulled her down next to him.

'We're going nowhere, Oliver,' she said. 'It's run its course.'

He tensed.

'It doesn't have to be like that.'

'Yes it does. It's time to go our separate ways. It was great while it lasted but it's become a distraction and let's be honest, it's never going to step up to the next stage, is it?'

An answer wasn't required. She finished putting her things

together and carried them through the side gate to stash them in her van. She glanced up as she closed the van door at the beautiful leafy frontage of the house. Finished now. Perfect. A garden to match the high spec of the house. And there was the problem right there.

In his eyes she would never be good enough to live somewhere so gorgeous. She was good enough to park her van outside, good enough to stop over, share his bed and be peripheral to his real life, but she would never be any more than that.

He trailed in her wake. A few of her belongings were inside his house, some clothes, a spare pair of shoes. She mentally threw them away. Position made clear, dignity wouldn't allow her to go back now. She opened the driver's door.

'Where are you going?' he said, an undertone of disbelief tinging his voice.

'I'm seeing my friends tonight and then I need to put some time into planning my next job,' she said, not looking at him. She climbed into the van.

'What about the white house job?'

'I'm perfectly capable of sourcing my own business,' she said. 'I've got a number of people waiting on start dates.'

Truth be told, she'd been less than her usual obsessive self about lining up work this last month. Letting standards slip, eye off the ball. Maybe this was for the best, a wake-up call she needed to quit a diversion that could never go anywhere.

He put himself between the open door and the van to stop her slamming it.

'I never said you weren't capable,' he said. 'I thought you'd be pleased.'

'Thing is, Oliver, I've been neglecting the business a bit these past few weeks. Best now if we call it a day.' She took a fortifying breath. 'It was just a bit of fun after all.'

She turned the key in the ignition and started the engine.

'You're saying you don't want to see me again?'

For a lawyer he was slow on the uptake.

'Yes,' she said. 'That's exactly what I'm saying. It was fun while it lasted.'

'I thought we had something pretty good.'

She stared out through the windscreen, her throat burning with the effort of swallowing tears. She shook her head and allowed herself one last glance up at him.

'Actually it was something pretty shallow,' she said, putting the van in gear. 'And now it's something that's over with.'

She drove away without looking back.

CHAPTER 10

Izzy shifted from foot to foot, waiting on the delivery of a load of gravel to rake over the newly-laid paving.

So it turned out Shauna had been right all along. A no-strings fling could only work if it was anonymous.

Throw yourself into work, Izzy, that's right. Always worked before. Parents a nightmare? Chuck yourself into work, the more hours the better. Boyfriend is a serial one-night-stander when he's supposedly working towards your future? No worries, take on some extra contracts. See if you can't work seven days a week. Oops, your own no-strings fling starts to corrupt your work ethic? No problem, get back to work and keep your eye on the prize.

Once she'd worked out what the prize was now, of course. Not a deposit on a house and a family with Joe. Not anymore. And not to have as good and inhibited a time as you can with Oliver.

Just what the hell did she want?

She didn't know. All she knew was she was totally and consumingly miserable. And for the first time ever, work simply wasn't cutting the mustard as a distraction.

***

Oliver stared at his laptop screen, rereading the same email for the fifth time without taking a word of it in.

First had come incredulity. Had she really knocked him back?

Hot on its heels had come defensiveness.

There had never been any more to it than just a fling for her, then. Used to making a swift exit from his casual dates, letting girls down swiftly and efficiently, the way she'd simply dispensed with him rankled. Vaguely insulted, he told himself he'd had a lucky escape, he didn't need to end it on his terms, that was stupid self-indulgence. That it was ended was enough.

For a day or two that approach worked. Iron stubbornness held out as he threw himself with renewed vigor into work, taking on new cases, building his workload back up to breaking point, just as he'd cut it back these last few weeks as he told himself he needed a bit of breathing space, in reality because he wanted to spend more time with Izzy. He could see now that this thing between them had started seeping into his life, encroaching on his work focus. He'd been denying it to himself, believing that he was keeping things separate.

Work was one thing. Home was another. Every time he looked out into the perfect garden he missed her even more. He'd fallen short of what she wanted, what she needed. He was his father's son after all.

Izzy was the one who'd had the lucky escape, not him.

That she refused to remain in a situation that wasn't working for her made her somehow all the more appealing. With a childhood spent watching his mother hold everything together, letting her life slip by while his father did whatever he liked, the last thing he found attractive in a woman was a doormat. Someone who danced to his tune made him run for the hills. Yet they always had until now.

Wasn't that what had hooked him from the outset? Her initial detachment that first night came back to him. Her crazy ground rules. He'd only found her again after that night by chance. And he knew she wouldn't change her mind now – she'd proved that the first time they met when she'd blown him away just by walking away. To be pursued by a woman was an instant turnoff, to the point where any interest shown by her made him run a mile in the opposite direction. Yet that had always happened. Until her.

For the first time he acknowledged to himself that he wanted more, and it scared the hell out of him.

He glanced around his sitting room. Everything in its place, showhome-perfect. So quiet he could hear the clock on the high mantelpiece ticking. Material reassuring evidence that he'd made it, that he was safe, was everywhere he looked. Just having it had always been enough, but now what was the point of any of it without her to share it?

He stood up and grabbed his keys. He wanted, *needed* to see her again and leaving it to Izzy or to chance would be pointless. Neither was going to act on his behalf anytime soon. If he wanted her back he'd have to take control of the situation himself.

***

The beginning of a new project.

Usually Izzy's favourite part of the job, outdone only by the end result when she could hand back a finished garden to its owners and let go. A bigger project this time than the courtyard garden she'd designed for Oliver. Less intimate, more showy, with less of her own personal taste influencing it. Oliver had pretty much given her free creative rein and...

She slapped him out of her mind by forcing her eyes to focus on the agreed spec diagram in front of her. Left unchecked he filtered back into her thoughts in seconds. She was determined that would soon cease with time and a bit of willpower. She turned a page of her plans and moved down the garden. Water feature was going to be about halfway down, to the left. She ran through the work in her mind.

A sound behind her. Clearly not the occupants of the house.

Both were at work, having entrusted her a key. She'd left the side gate open, waiting for the couple of student labourers she used on an ad hoc basis, perfect for the hard graft needed to clear and prepare the site at the outset.

She turned, ready to tell them to get started at the end of the garden where a decrepit old rotting shed needed dismantling and throwing in the skip out front, and her mouth closed with a snap.

How the hell was she supposed to stop him filtering his way into her thoughts when he didn't even have the decency to steer clear of her physically?

She sighed.

'Oliver. You can't just turn up here. This is private property.'

'I need to talk to you.'

His voice. The voice she loved that kept her awake at night. She deliberately didn't look into the hazel eyes, afraid it would remind her of the times she'd looked there before, their bodies entwined, his mouth against hers. She needed to forget what was past. What was gone.

'I'm busy,' she said.

Keep it professional, Izzy. Work tones.

'I'm starting this job this morning. I'm in the middle of setting up. I don't have time for small talk.'

'It's important.'

She rounded on him then. Important now, was it? Not something to be fitted around more significant parts of his life? Not an afterthought?

Let him be fitted in for once.

She made a point of flipping through a couple of pages of her neatly-written plans, glancing down the garden as if totally preoccupied with her work.

'My labourers will be here any moment to rip that shed down and start clearing out rubbish. I don't have time for this. We've said all there was to say, you made your point of view totally clear.'

She offered him a brief parting smile.

'Goodbye, Oliver. Could you close the gate on your way out, please?'

She began to walk down the garden. Please let him just go. Please. Her heart wanted to rush into his arms. Her head was still busy feeling cheap at the way he viewed her, knowing she'd encouraged that. Her head won, easily. Her heart was too fragile to be in with a chance. She couldn't rely on it anymore. She never should have.

'I came to say I'm sorry,' he called after her.

She stopped walking. Looked down at her feet and took a deep calming breath before turning back to him.

'What exactly are you sorry for, Oliver?' she said. 'We had a good time and now it's over. We both knew what we were getting into – right?'

'I miss you. I miss what we had.'

What we had. There was exactly the point. No intimation still that he wanted any more than that. He'd had his playtime taken away and he didn't like it.

'We had hot sex,' she said. She pasted a bright I-don't-care smile on to emphasise her point.

She watched him close his eyes briefly. Obviously exasperated that she wasn't just coming back running.

'It was more than that,' he said.

'Of course. I'd forgotten the dinners and the chat. Obviously hoops you felt you had to jump through in order to *get to* the hot sex.' She gave him a smile. 'I'm not complaining, Oliver. I went into it with my eyes wide open. And at the beginning that was what I wanted too.'

'At the beginning?'

She ran a hand distractedly through her hair.

'The thing is, Oliver, this just doesn't feel like fun to me anymore. It feels cheap, like I'm some bit on the side like that brassy woman who showed up on my parent's doorstep all those years ago.'

He walked down the garden and grabbed her hand. Her stomach

fluttered in response.

'This is not the same thing at all. You are not some bit on the side, as you call it. I'm not like your father. I don't have a wife or partner, I don't have a family.'

'You don't have a wife or family, no,' she said.' You have your work, your ambitions, some stupid misplaced drive that means you'll never quit until you've made a billion or conquered the universe. You have this whole other life that nothing else penetrates. I want to share it but it's No Admittance. I don't even know what it is that you're so desperately working towards, but whatever it is you're striving for, Oliver, you're going to end up achieving it on your own. And where's the enjoyment of that without someone to share it with?' She took her hand away from his. 'I'm sorry if you think I'm being unfair, if you think I'm moving the goalposts. When I met you a fling really was all I wanted. No strings, no comeback. But now I know I want to be with someone who shares their whole life with me, not just the scraps they can spare. We want different things, you and I. It was fun while it lasted but it's over.'

'I didn't come here to ask you to reconsider.'

She stared at him. Then what the hell was this about?

'You didn't?'

'What I said to you was totally crass, I realise that now. Lining up a contract so we could carry on the way we were. Truth is, I was too afraid to ask you to stay properly so I tried to find a way of holding onto you that didn't have any risk.'

She looked at him, not speaking.

He raked both hands through his hair.

'Izzy, my father was a layabout. I'm not sure he ever did an honest day's work in his whole life. My mother worked two jobs, sometimes three, so that she could keep things together. She claimed what state benefits she could, and as the eldest I was responsible for cooking and looking out for my kid brother when she wasn't around. We were always short of money, robbing Peter to pay Paul but my father had no problem spending the household budget at the pub. We were in a vicious circle that my mother could never break out of on her own.'

'Your mother stuck by him?' she asked.

He nodded.

'There was something about him that made her take him back again and again. She had this inner optimism that somehow he might change. He'd show up, telling her he had the promise of a new job, that things would be different, and it would last a few weeks, maybe a month before he fell out with his boss, or he began to take days off, and then the job would disappear and we'd be back to square one.'

'So are they still together now?'

She was thinking of her own parents – stick it out until the end, happy or not.

He shook his head.

'Eventually when my brother and I left home, she drew a line under it. As if she'd given him chance after chance because of us. Once we'd gone I think the motivation went with us and she decided to cut her losses at last. I don't blame her. I think she should have jumped ship much earlier.'

He gave her a small smile. 'I didn't have much time for my father, we've talked about that before. But what he has given me is a strong work ethic. I never feel like I've done enough, there's always this nagging fear that the rug will be pulled out from under me and I'll lose everything. And after what my mother went through I never wanted to take anyone along for that ride. In case...'

He paused and swallowed hard, she heard the click in his throat. And suddenly she understood him.

'In case you turn out like him?' she asked gently.

He didn't answer and didn't look up at her.

'Oliver, just because he behaved that way doesn't make it a physical trait. You don't even belong in that world anymore, I mean look at your house, your job, your car. He chose to drift through life without a purpose. It was a choice, not a character flaw. You've chosen a totally different path. Maybe he *did* inspire you, just not in the way you wanted. Reverse psychology. Do you think you would have achieved all you have if he'd been a better father? Maybe you'd have ended up a different person, someone complacent. Maybe you would have drifted through life directionless if your father had been Joe Average. You shouldn't have regrets like that, it's destructive.' She paused. 'For what it's worth, you seem to have turned out pretty well to me.'

'I know my work ethic is crazy. The odd thing is, the first time in years that I've lightened up has been these last few weeks, knowing that you were at home. I shifted work around so I could make sure I was home for dinner. So I could see you. I realised I was looking forward to ending my day with you.'

'In bed,' she said, face neutral.

He clenched his hands.

'Izzy, please, it's *not* just about the sex. It never was. Right from the beginning I was trying to convince myself that it was because that made it safe, made it something I could walk away from, something where no one took any risk of getting hurt. But the more I got to know you the more it's become about being with you, talking to you, spending time with you, getting to know you.'

He looked up at her and the anguish in his eyes pulled at her heart.

'I was too scared that I'd end up ruining everything to even acknowledge there was something between us worth keeping.'

'You said you didn't come here to ask me to reconsider,' she said. 'So what did you come here for?'

There was a pause.

'I came to ask you on a date,' he said.

A surprised burst of laughter bubbled up inside her.

'A date?' She could hear the incredulity in her own voice.

He raised his eyebrows with a hint of defensiveness.

'Yes, a date. You know the kind of thing – I pick you up, I bring flowers, we go out somewhere nice, get to know each other, enjoy each other's company. And at the end of the evening, I drop you home.'

She stared at him.

'Home?'

He nodded.

'To your place. If you like. I guess what I'm really saying is that we skipped that whole stage, didn't we? Went straight from not knowing each other to bed. OK so we've gone about it all backwards, but so what? Let's start over.'

Could it really be that easy?

'You can't just go back and fill in the blanks like that and expect it all to work,' she said. 'It would be like me laying a lawn or planting up beds here without putting all the groundwork in first. It might look great on the surface, might even last a little while. But eventually it would all just wilt and die off. You can't build something that will last by skipping to the end.'

'You don't know that. Just give it a try.'

'Then what?'

'Then we just see how it goes.'

'It?'

'Us. I want there to be an Us. I want that not to be an after-thought or a side effect or a quick fuck or one night stand. I'm in love with you.'

She looked at him in shock that he'd used the L-word. The expression on his face was open, his desire to make this work palpable. She had been wronged girlfriend and other woman. Maybe this time she could try and combine the two.

'You're serious?'

'Absolutely serious. No secrets, no lies...' he swallowed '... no putting work first. A proper relationship. You and me. How about it?'

Excitement simmer through her, slowly at first then gathering pace.

'Ground rules,' she began and he pulled her against him and

pressed his forehead against hers.

'Not a bloody chance,' he said.